ASSASSIN

Gunfire ripped ... instant the armed men lost their line of sight to Cameron.

John was on his feet, grabbing Harry's arm as he overturned the table for some sort of cover. The lines of fans dissolved in screaming panic, some people even blundering into the line of fire. The assassins now raised their aim a bit, shooting over the fans' heads to force everyone to duck down and give them a clear field to fire again.

Huddled behind the table, Harry flung a pleading glance to the roped-off area behind him, where Thomas stood. He could read minds—why hadn't he seen this coming? Why wasn't he moving to stop it? The giant maintained a pose of readiness, but he didn't move. He seemed to be waiting for something. With sick realization, Sturdley understood what the giant was waiting for.

My God he thought. We've been set up.

Harry's voice rose in a scream, trying to pierce the chaos around them, "John—we've got to Rift out of here!"

STAN LEE'S RIFTWORLD VILLAINS

ROC

SCIENCE FICTION AND FANTASY

☐ **THE STALK by Janet and Chris Morris.** The Unity had made its offer, stated its terms. Now the United Nations of Earth must respond. But how could Mickey Croft make an unbiased decision for all humankind, when his own direct contact with the Interpreter had left him uncertain whether he himself was still completely human? (453077—$4.99)

☐ **DOWN AMONG THE DEAD MEN by Simon R. Green.** It was the most ancient of evils—and it was about to wake—in this sequel to *Blue Moon Rising.* "This one really stands out from the crowd."—*Science Fiction Chronicle* (453018—$4.50)

☐ **RED BRIDE by Christopher Fowler.** A horror is on the loose, savagely killing again and again. The police are powerless to stop the slaughter. The finest detectives cannot unmask the killer. Only one man suspects the secret. (452933—$4.99)

☐ **STALKER ANALOG by Mel Odom.** Bethany Shay was a cop on a serial killer's trail—a trail that led from the Church to the cybernet and into the heart of madness. (452577—$5.50)

☐ **THE MISTS FROM BEYOND *20 Ghost Stories & Tales From the Other Side* by Peter Straub, Clive Barker, Joyce Carol Oates and 17 others.** Twenty of the most haunting ghost tales ever created . . . all of them certain to transport you, if only for a brief time, from our everyday world to one in which even the faintest of shadows takes on a ghostly life of its own. (452399—$20.00)

*Prices slightly higher in Canada

Buy them at your local bookstore or use this convenient coupon for ordering.

PENGUIN USA
P.O. Box 999 — Dept. #17109
Bergenfield, New Jersey 07621

Please send me the books I have checked above.
I am enclosing $__________ (please add $2.00 to cover postage and handling). Send check or money order (no cash or C.O.D.'s) or charge by Mastercard or VISA (with a $15.00 minimum). Prices and numbers are subject to change without notice.

Card #__________ Exp. Date __________
Signature__________
Name__________
Address__________
City __________ State __________ Zip Code __________

For faster service when ordering by credit card call **1-800-253-6476**

Allow a minimum of 4-6 weeks for delivery. This offer is subject to change without notice.

Stan Lee's

RIFTWORLD

Volume Two

VILLAINS

by Bill McCay

A ROC BOOK

ROC
Published by the Penguin Group
Penguin Books USA Inc., 375 Hudson Street,
New York, New York 10014, U.S.A.
Penguin Books Ltd, 27 Wrights Lane,
London W8 5TZ, England
Penguin Books Australia Ltd, Ringwood,
Victoria, Australia
Penguin Books Canada Ltd, 10 Alcorn Avenue,
Toronto, Ontario, Canada M4V 3B2
Penguin Books (N.Z.) Ltd, 182–190 Wairau Road,
Auckland 10, New Zealand

Penguin Books Ltd, Registered Offices:
Harmondsworth, Middlesex, England,

First published by Roc, an imprint of Dutton Signet,
a division of Penguin Books USA Inc.

First Printing, February, 1994
10 9 8 7 6 5 4 3 2 1

Copyright © Byron Preiss Visual Publications, Inc., 1994
Cover painting, interior illustrations, and cover copyright © Byron Preiss Visual Publications, Inc., 1994

Afterword copyright © Stan Lee, 1994
Stan Lee's Riftworld is a trademark of
Byron Preiss Visual Publication, Inc.

Illustrations by Dave Gibbons
Cover by Bruce Jensen
Edited by Howard Zimmerman
Design by Dean Motter
A Byron Preiss Visual Publications, Inc. Book

All rights reserved. For information address Byron Preiss Visual Publications, Inc.
24 West 25th Street, 11th Floor, New York, New York, 10010.

REGISTERED TRADEMARK—MARCA REGISTRADA

Printed in the United States of America

Without limiting the rights under copyright reserved above, no part of this publication may be reproduced, stored in or introduced into a retrieval system, or transmitted, in any form, or by any means (electronic, mechanical, photocopying, recording, or otherwise), without the prior written permission of both the copyright owner and the above publisher of this book.

BOOKS ARE AVAILABLE AT QUANTITY DISCOUNTS WHEN USED TO PROMOTE PRODUCTS OR SERVICES. FOR INFORMATION PLEASE WRITE TO PREMIUM MARKETING DIVISION, PENGUIN BOOKS USA INC., 375 HUDSON STREET, NEW YORK, NEW YORK 10014.

If you purchased this book without a cover you should be aware that this book is stolen property. It was reported as "unsold and destroyed" to the publisher and neither the author nor the publisher has received any payment for this "stripped book."

THE STORY THUS FAR

In *Crossover,* "Happy" Harry Sturdley, publisher of the Fantasy Factory comics company, wished for something new to capture his readers' imaginations . . . like real live superheroes. And aspiring artist John Cameron had just the talent to make it happen. With his unique ability to manipulate the Rift, Cameron brought in fifty twenty-foot-tall giants, each with superior physical and mental powers.

Though Cameron had misgivings, Sturdley rushed to get the giants under exclusive contract, to chronicle their adventures in comics. The giants found themselves donning white Spandex uniforms designed by Fantasy Factory artists and patrolling the city. They were instantly hailed as national crime fighters, and their comics were runaway bestsellers.

But it all got out of hand with Operation Hero when the giants cleaned the streets of criminals, unintentionally driving them underground into the subways, where no hero could follow. The subways were in chaos, and it wasn't much better aboveground. One giant nearly battered a car thief to death and then turned on the human witnesses.

Detained by the Immigration and Naturalization Service in lower Manhattan for hiring illegal aliens, Sturdley received a clandestine visit from one of the giants. He began to warn Sturdley of something of great importance when he was attacked and dragged off into the night. Though taken aback at the strange incident and still behind bars, Sturdley remained the heroes' biggest fan.

From Harry Sturdley's airborne perspective, midtown Manhattan stretched out like a demented crazy quilt. The designer didn't show a flair for color, as the high-rise rooftops were a uniform gray-black. But the streams of traffic in the streets between made for multicolored piping.

Flying west over Rockefeller Center, Sturdley banked right at Park Avenue and veered south. He swooped closer to the ground, skimming over the lower office buildings. His cape flapped behind him in the slipstream, and he allowed a toothy grin to light up the planes and angles of his lean face.

Waving to the occasional rooftop sunbather, Sturdley zoomed along to the upper Twenties, zeroing in on the building that housed his comic-book company, the Fantasy Factory.

That's when he noticed the crowd gathered in the street below.

"Look!" someone cried as he swooped down, "up in the sky—it's *Sturdley*!"

Glancing down at the royal blue *S* on the chest of his ultra-tight yellow unitard, Sturdley smiled. It paid to advertise. "What's the problem, citizens?" he asked the nervous crowd as he landed lightly amid them.

"There's a giant on the loose," a kid at the outskirts of the group said. "He's busting up everything!"

"Fear not," Sturdley said, slipping into hero-speak. "I'll handle that."

With the aid of his superpowers, Sturdley soon located the rampaging giant. But he halted in midair when he recognized the villain. "*Robert*—what do you think you're doing?"

The twenty-foot-tall visitor from another world had broken off a streetlight and was using it like a baseball bat to smash windows. His chiseled features were perfect hero material, but the sneer that swept over his face when he saw Harry Sturdley was pure evil.

"I don't answer to you, little man," Robert snarled. "I'll swat you out of the air like a bug." Clutching the light pole two-handed, he swung it with all of his considerable strength.

"I'm protected!" Sturdley cried, and as he extended his right arm a shield magically appeared. It was only eleven inches wide and seventeen inches tall, and seemed paper thin. But it withstood Robert's blows, rocking the giant back.

Sturdley glanced down at the face of the shield, checking for damage. It was fine, except for a dent in the portion that read, ". . . the party of the second part shall hold harmless—"

"That miserable contract is no defense!" Robert roared. He glared at Sturdley's shield, his eyes suddenly glowing a brilliant, piercing red. Dazzling crimson beams shot from his eye sockets, striking the shield, which began to smolder.

"What the hell is this?" Sturdley protested. "You don't have *heat vision.* Where did you pick that up?

Have you been hanging around with those jokers from Dynasty Comics?"

The contract/shield suddenly burst into flames. So did Sturdley's uniform, his cape, and then his whole body. Sturdley plummeted to earth, engulfed in flames.

The worst of his death agonies, though, was Robert's mocking laughter.

Sturdley moaned in his sleep, shifting on the thin foam mattress in the otherwise empty detention cell. His hands moved instinctively, striving to beat out imaginary flames.

CHAPTER 1

"Now *that's* more like the Robert I used to know," Barbara purred. Sunlight filtering through the treetops dappled her nude, Amazonian form—a form nearly twenty feet long.

The two giants lay in the midst of a circle of devastation in the woods of upper Westchester. Their lovemaking had been passionate, energetic—and rough on the local landscape.

"So impetuous." Barbara stretched like a satisfied cat, a lazy smile on her generous lips. "Like the times back home when we used to steal off into the forests."

Robert's chiseled features hardened. "This is completely different from our old holdings in the woods. And the stakes are higher than becoming a mere Master of Masters." His hand seized her shoulder in a painful grip. "We could be Masters of a whole world, a domain larger than your father could ever had imagined." His lips twisted. "If we're not betrayed."

Abruptly he rose and began gathering their scattered clothing. It still felt strange to don the skintight white costumes Harry Sturdley had created for them.

Robert's lips twitched into a wolfish grin as he watched the play of muscles in Barbara's back and buttocks as she wriggled the costume up her long legs, the white cloth making a startling contrast with her allover tan. She turned, raising her arms to don the top of the costume, light and shadow playing across the tautness of her sculpted breasts.

Sturdley would have a seizure if he saw her this way, Robert thought—it would probably transgress some part of his precious Comics Code.

Robert's face tightened as he slipped on his own clothes. Sturdley had been useful, teaching Robert as much as he needed to know about this strange society of Lessers without Masters. But already Robert was moving to end the little man's control over the heroes, as Sturdley had named them. He'd banked on Sturdley accepting that, as long as the Lesser could make money with his comic books.

But if Sturdley came to fear Robert's people and their long-range plans, if he actively sought to hinder them . . .

Yanking his Spandex top into place, he turned to the now fully dressed Barbara. "Let's go and see Gideon," he said curtly.

A short walk brought them out of the deeper woods and into a small clearing where a large tree had fallen, tearing a hole in the canopy of green. Gideon's arms had been stretched behind him, bent round the trunk of the fallen forest giant, and tied in place.

Barbara gasped in the sight of the renegade's face, bruised and swollen from repeated blows. Back home, most of their kind would have offered submission long before enduring such a beating. As soon as the mental aura that protected them weakened enough for blows actually to land on their bodies, most would surrender. But Gideon had fought on, valiantly, hopelessly, until he'd been knocked unconscious.

Thomas and another guard who had been sitting in the shadows of the trees rose to their feet. They were fully clad in white hero suits.

"Robert." Gideon's voice came out more like a croak. "How nice of you to think of me, considering all your other distractions." The prisoner turned bold, bruised eyes toward Barbara.

For a second, the world dissolved in red rage as Robert stepped forward to send a backhanded blow across Gideon's mocking face. "You runt of a traitor—"

Fresh blood leaked from Gideon's split lips, dripping onto the tattered, filthy remains of his white costume. "Sturdley is a good man," he said, each word an effort. "He deserved a warning of your true intentions."

"Not that he listened to you," Robert mocked. "He now thinks you climbed to his prison cell to kill him. Sturdley is blinded by greed. Without even realizing it, he serves *me*."

"And what do you serve?" Gideon shot back. "What code do you follow? You hold me prisoner. When was that ever an accepted practice back home?"

"This isn't home," Robert began.

"No! It's a place where we could make a new beginning! We have much to offer the people here—and they have much to offer us."

" 'People?' " Thomas inquired disdainfully. "You mean Lessers, runt. And I take what I want from Lessers."

"Yes, you could do that back home. But on this world, you're fifty against hundreds of millions. Don't you *feel* them? Whenever it's quiet, I hear the rustle of thousands—millions of consciousnesses—thinking, feeling, grieving, rejoicing. Don't you hear it?"

"Like the chittering of insects," Robert said dismissively.

"But these insects have weapons even you couldn't survive."

Robert sneered. "To turn those against us, they'd have to kill millions of their own people."

"If they're frightened enough, the humans will do that," Gideon said. "But it could be different."

"Don't you understand, runt?" Barbara shouted. "We don't want things to be different. We want them the way they *ought* to be!"

"I understand only too clearly," Gideon said in a frozen voice. The muscles on his chest contorted; there was a dull *snap*! and suddenly he leapt up from his place of imprisonment. It was so inconceivable, so unexpected, the giants stood frozen for a second.

That was enough time for Gideon to hurl himself, not into flight, but straight at Robert. His stature may have been small compared to the others, but he was incredibly agile. And in his hands he held the length of heavy rope that had bound him in place.

Gideon dodged around Robert, his arms upraised, displaying wrists that were banded by red, raw, galled wounds, oozing through cracks of crusted blood.

He must have been working at his bonds all night, Robert thought.

Then Gideon was past him, twisting the improvised garrote around Robert's neck.

The steady, inhuman pressure exerted by the rebel giant's hands crushed the rope against the guardian aura that protected Robert's body, forcing it inward until Robert felt the pressure of his own flesh. His fingers clawed against the rope as it began to choke him, but he could get no purchase on it. He wobbled on his feet, then sank to his knees, still plucking futilely.

Barbara cried out and took a step forward, but Thomas grabbed her wrist with a free hand, holding her back. Robert's chosen lieutenants, Thomas and Victor, stood where they were, calmly watching the combat through half-lidded eyes.

They're waiting to see if he takes me—then they'll take him, Robert thought. *A cold comfort.*

The garrote was sawing into Robert's throat, cutting off his air. His vision was becoming blurred. He got an impression of Barbara struggling to reach him again, but Thomas easily restrained her. *Another prize for the victors,* Robert thought bitterly.

He stopped clawing at the rope crushing his windpipe, and went for a more vulnerable spot, grappling for Gideon's wounded wrists. Robert heard the hiss of pain erupt from the would-be assassin, and he twisted his grip. Fresh blood burst from the chafed lesions, making Gideon's wrists slippery, the crimson liquid running down to stain the forearms of Robert's hero suit.

Teeth gritted, Robert wrenched, twisting at Gideon's injuries . . . and the grip on the garrote faltered.

Robert burst free of the length of rope, throwing a punch to the side of Gideon's head even as he sucked down blessed air.

Gideon punched back, but he didn't have the reach, power, or stamina of his opponent. With every breath he drew in, Robert got stronger, while Gideon grew steadily weaker as more blood escaped his wounded, battered body.

Robert slugged blow after blow to Gideon's midsection and face. The runt's protective aura was gone completely, yet somehow he remained on his feet.

This intransigence drove Robert into a blood-fury, his blows thudding home until his knuckles began to swell even through his own aura.

When Gideon finally dropped, Robert kicked his recumbent body, his buskins lashing into the fallen giant's stomach, sides, and back. His face a mask of insane rage, Robert raised a foot to stomp Gideon's head.

"Stop it!" a voice shouted in his ear. Hands grabbed at one arm, pulling him off-balance.

"You'll kill him!" Barbara cried. "We can't afford it!"

Snarling, he shook her away, but rational thought returned and the red veil of rage dissipated. There were too few of them on this world. He couldn't afford to reduce their numbers—not right now.

Robert turned to face Thomas and Victor, who watched the spectacular beating he'd administered, all thoughts of challenge now gone. Robert swallowed, his chest still heaving. *"I will rule!"* he spat at them. "Fix his wounds, then bind him again—securely this time."

Thomas and Victor quickly moved to obey like whipped curs.

Barbara sidled up to Robert, staring as if she'd seen him now for the first time. Dread sparkled in her eyes as she licked luscious, fear-dry lips. "Are you all right?" she asked hesitantly.

"Gods below!" he swore, grabbing her by the shoulders. Barbara staggered as he rested a considerable part of his weight on her.

"This cursed world," Robert muttered. "The voices

always scratching in my brain, the air tasting wrong . . ."

He stared down at the limp form on the ground.

What is this world doing to our people? he wondered.

CHAPTER 2

In his cell in downtown Manhattan, Harry Sturdley opened his eyes and realized he hadn't gone up in flames.

You weren't supposed to be able to feel yourself dying in dreams, he thought, drawing a ragged breath into his tight chest. He shifted, his back creaking a complaint about the thin mattress under him. This might be the best accommodation in the Immigration and Naturalization Service's detention center, but for Harry's money, INS had a lot to learn about comfort.

With a groan, he shifted to a sitting position on his bunk, a feeble shaft of daylight illuminating his stubbled face through the barred window of his cell.

Sturdley glanced down at the oversize orange jumpsuit the INS people had given him. This is why I couldn't beat Robert in my dream—the baggy uniform. As the Fantasy Factory's publisher and earliest resident genius, Sturdley had developed what he considered to be the laws of comic books. His first axiom: "The tighter the costume, the stronger the hero."

How could he be strong in a suit that looked like a deflated weather balloon?

His rules had been codified in simpler days, before "Happy" Harry had brought real superheroes to the streets of New York—and before the INS had arrested him for importing twenty-foot-tall illegal aliens from another world. Who'd have thought that weird kid John Cameron could control a doorway through space? But then, who'd have expected *any* of the stuff that had happened in the last month or so?

Harry got off the bunk and went to the cell door. "Anybody out there?" he called. "Can I at least find out what's going on?"

Alone now in the detention center's lounge, Harry watched the TV news. The First News broadcast had him squirming with embarrassment.

When he'd realized he was about to be arrested, Sturdley had arranged what he thought would be a surefire plan to get himself released. Operation Hero, a twenty-four-hour all-out war on crime, would use the fifty newly arrived giants as a vigilante superforce. After seventeen hours of action, Operation Hero had succeeded, at least in part. Senator Al DeMagogua and a lot of other New Yorkers now loved the giants.

But the operation had turned those places inaccessible to twenty-footers—like New York's infamous subways—into lawless hellholes. If the reports were to be believed, every criminal with half a brain had moved his activities underground.

"It would've worked in the comics," Harry muttered to himself.

Sturdley was glad to turn away from the screen when he was told he had visitors. Frank McManus, the head of the Fantasy Factory's legal department, entered the lounge. The lawyer's jowly face looked tired and a little shell-shocked as he opened a briefcase and began removing papers.

"Good news, Harry," he announced. "You're out of here."

Sturdley looked over to the man who accompanied McManus, solidly built, imposing Ira Orreck, a high-priced criminal attorney. "Did you manage to pull this off?"

Orreck shook his head. "The politicians were moving that way anyhow. We know the Police Benevolent Association was behind the illegal alien charges in the first place. They were afraid your superheroes would put them out of business. Well, Operation Hero has proven that the city will still need cops."

"At least in the subways," McManus put in with a grin. "Anyway, the Immigration people have decided to let you go, pending further investigation."

An INS guard came in carrying a plastic bag full of Harry's clothes and personal effects.

"So," Harry Sturdley said in satisfaction, "Operation Hero worked after all."

"In a manner of speaking," Orreck finally said. "Your boy Robert called the mayor this morning with the perfect threat."

Sturdley turned a puzzled face to the lawyer. "What did he say?"

McManus' grin grew larger. "He told the mayor that as long as you were incarcerated he intended to continue Operation Hero."

Marty Burke shifted between the black satin sheets on his bed, watching *The First News Morning Report* and its coverage of Operation Hero.

"Well, Kara Jane," anchorman Brad Borsman said with his patented synthetic smile, "let's see what's happening live from the battle lines."

The scene shifted to the blond figure of Leslie Ann Nasotrudere in her First News blazer, her microphone ready as she led a camera crew down into the Twenty-third Street IRT station. The camera followed her fashion-model silhouette as she spoke. "We're watching a process of reclamation here, Brad." The focus shifted as the camera moved past her to pan beyond the token booth turnstiles and onto the subway platform. "A mixed task force of NYPD and Transit Authority police just went down to clear the station. The plan is to seal the East Side line both above and below Union Square with converging police battalions—"

A skirmish line of officers in blue moved along the platform.

Suddenly a figure darted from under one of the benches for commuters and scuttled for the tracks. It was human, but moved with the uncanny speed of a giant waterbug. The figure, in shorts and a torn T-shirt, dropped off the platform and ran for the darkness of the tunnel. In the background, yells of "Police! Freeze!" joined muffled cursing as the officers milled around, some chasing him, some covering other shadowy nooks where undesirables might hide.

It looked like an outtake from the Keystone Kops, but Leslie Ann's perfect face maintained its serious frown, as if she were afraid of cracking her makeup. "This is the first time the police have been down here in almost twelve hours," she went on, "since the shocking outbreak of complete lawlessness in the transit system brought on by the aboveground vigilantism of Operation Hero."

Burke had to smile at the inserted editorial comment. Harry Sturdley had been behind the hoopla that turned the alien giants into heroes, and he'd crossed swords with Leslie Ann Nasotrudere at a press conference when she tried to lead a media backlash against the giant superheroes.

Sturdley had won that battle, embarrassing Leslie Ann, but gained a relentless enemy for himself and, by extension, for the heroes. It had also solidified the tie between her and Marty Burke. He had higher ambitions than being the second-greatest genius at the Fantasy Factory. In meeting after meeting, Burke had championed a new wave of artists, only to clash with Sturdley's archaic ideas of what comics characters should be.

The old man should step aside—and if he wouldn't move, he'd be forced out. Then Marty Burke would run the company as it *ought* to be run. To accomplish that, Burke needed allies—and he'd found one in the newswoman trying to bring Sturdley down. She had approached him, something had clicked, and . . .

Burke shook his head, watching Leslie Ann continue her live newsfeed. He had seen the woman behind the professional mask. This hard-nosed investigative reporter was the same waif who had dragged herself into his apartment at three in the morning, her clothing stained and rumpled, her eyes sunken with fatigue. It was hard to believe that the image on the screen had anything to do with the vulnerable young woman who had lain naked in his arms, crying bitterly because a bystander had tried to grab her microphone during a live broadcast that night.

Then, despite the hour and her fatigue, Leslie Ann had proved to be a passionate and demanding lover. Burke was not used to the pressure of having to give two live performances a day—let alone in an hour—and he had a hard time keeping up. Leslie Ann

Nasotrudere might be a complicated personality, but Marty knew there was one thing he could depend on. She wanted Harry Sturdley's scalp. And if she got it, Burke thought, *I* might just wind up running the Fantasy Factory.

Burke got a nasty shock moments after he arrived at the Fantasy Factory offices. He headed down the hallway to executive row, intending to have a heart-to-heart chat with the chief editor, Bob Gunnar. With Sturdley out of the way, there were some ideas he wanted to float . . .

He was almost to Gunnar's door when Peg Faber looked up from her desk. "Marty, I was just about to call you," Sturdley's redheaded assistant said. She was a cute little thing, with curves in all the right places, but she'd nearly broken his arm when he'd expressed some interest after a few beers. Broads who knew karate belonged in comic books, not out in the real world where they would damage valuable artists' assets.

"There's a meeting for the senior staff in half an hour," she said.

Burke nodded. He should have expected Gunnar to go the management-by-committee route. Now there'd be no chance to put his ideas across quietly. But he *might* put them across noisily, with the aid of senior editor Thad Westmoreland and the clique of young artists.

At that moment, the door behind Peg swung open, and Harry Sturdley strode out. His hair was damp from the in-office shower, and he'd changed his clothes. "I know it's not in your job description, Peg," he said, "but could you get these clothes I wore in jail off to the cleaners? Either that, or burn them."

"W-when did you get out?" Burke burst into the conversation.

"Oh, I've been here for hours," Sturdley told him. "I'm surprised your girlfriend Leslie Ann didn't report it to you."

The meeting of the Fantasy Factory's brain trust had a surprising number of empty chairs. Several artists and editors—especially the ones from Brooklyn—hadn't come to work thanks to the chaos in the subways. At least half of the people who did appear for the meeting were astonished to see Sturdley out of the clink. Even Marty Burke's group of would-be mutineers was subdued.

Happy Harry smiled at his troops. Young Zeb Grantfield, whose forte was big-busted, slim-hipped superbabes, was seated a little distance from Burke and his cronies. Good. Perhaps the clique was breaking up. Old warhorse illustrator Fabian Thibault was whispering with Mack Nagel. Now there was an interesting case. Nagel had done hack work in old horror comics for years without any real success. He'd ended up begging Sturdley for a job, and Harry had paired Nagel with Grantfield, hoping the elderly artist's professionalism would rub off on his wayward wonderkid. Instead, Nagel had picked up Grantfield's hot-babe technique, and was now the artist on their second heroes comic, *The Fantastic Barbara.* The oldest artist on the staff was now the hottest new fan favorite.

Sturdley continued to smile as he glanced around the conference table. Not so long ago, Burke and his crew had a lock on the Fantasy Factory's hot titles: Reece Yantsey did *Schizodroid,* the hero with a thousand faces, personalities, and powers; Grantfield drew *Jumboy,* the spin-off, bad-attitude super-giant; and

Burke himself provided scripts and art for *Mr. Pain.* Even Sturdley had to admire Burke's work on that title. The character, a superhero created in a brain-surgery accident (he received super-fast reflexes at the cost of most of his sensory nerves), was in a rut. Burke had rung in some major changes, and made the book a bestseller.

Of course, it had also provided Burke with a nearly unassailable power base. That is, until Sturdley got a licensing contract with the newly arrived giants. Now comicdom's hottest-selling items were books about real, live heroes—Nagel's *The Fantastic Barbara* and John Cameron's *The Amazing Robert.*

A late arrival opened the conference room door—Elvio Vital, the Mexican-born artist who drew the Fantasy Factory's only humor book, *The Electrocutioner.* Besides being almost supernaturally quick at the drawing board, Elvio was a natural peacemaker. Sturdley noticed that he headed immediately to midtable to sit by John Cameron.

"Okay," Sturdley said, calling them to order. "I know this meeting is a surprise, but I'm sure you've figured out *why* I called it. We need to plan our moves in the light of the latest events."

"You mean, thanks to the uproar you created with this half-assed Operation Hero fiasco." Burke leapt to the attack. "You unleashed your pet giants to wreak havoc on New York City until you got out of jail. The only problem is, the Fantasy Factory will be held responsible. If we start getting sued for damages, the whole company will go down the tubes—and it's *your fault!*"

A worried buzz made its way around the table, but

Harry had expected that. "Let's see what our legal department has to say. Frank?"

Frank McManus rose from his chair, ready with the opinion he'd been working on since Sturdley had hatched the Operation Hero idea. "The heroes are not employees of the Fantasy Factory, *per se.* I don't believe we stand in any legal danger."

"But our public image is in lots of danger," Burke said, shifting his ground. "In the eyes of the public, those giants are huge, tangible symbols of the Fantasy Factory. You've been braying about them to any reporter who'll still listen. You've tied us to them, and now they're tied to all the disasters that happened on the subways, not to mention the reports of thuglike behavior from some of the heroes."

"If you listened to anything besides *First News,* maybe you'd be more aware of the public's reaction," Sturdley shot back. "In the International News Combine/Gallup overnight poll, pro-hero sentiment was over sixty percent. More important from our point of view is the response in the comics market."

He turned to Yvette Zelcerre, the petite head of publicity and marketing. "The phones have been ringing off the hook since yesterday afternoon," she said in her slightly accented voice. "Based on the further demand this morning, I suggest that we not only immediately go back to press for both *Robert* and *Barbara* Number One, but we should triple the print runs from what we'd planned."

An excited buzz ran round the table. The potential royalty payments for Mack Nagel and John Cameron had just risen astronomically. Sturdley watched the greed and consternation on the faces of Burke's coterie. Their stock had just gone down big-time.

"I . . . I'd like to suggest a Schizodroid-Robert team-up." Reece Yantsey managed to make himself heard over the babble.

Sturdley shook his head. "No way."

"Then how about teaming him up with Maurice?" Yantsey pressed, willing to settle for Robert's less photogenic sidekick.

Again Sturdley shook his head. "We can't do it," he said. "There's a clause in the licensing contract. The heroes will not appear in the Fantasy Factory galaxy. We only fictionalize their actual adventures."

Sturdley kept a straight face, but he wanted to gloat. He had inserted that clause to keep the jackals like Yantsey from using the heroes to sell their books.

His announcement caused a new outburst as the other artists realized they wouldn't be able to hook their wagons to the giants' star. "It was strictly business," Sturdley said.

"But putting business aside for a second, we still have a problem with the heroes."

All eyes went to the middle of the table, where John Cameron had stood up. The kid's voice was quiet, but somehow he made it heard above the uproar. "They did a lot of good things yesterday and last night. But there were problems—big problems. I saw one of the giants, Thomas, go berserk on a car thief yesterday. He was flinging him up in the air, then barely catching him. When he finally let the thief down, the guy tried to crawl away. Thomas nearly killed him with a couple of openhanded blows."

The whole room went silent. This was like hearing the pope expressing doubts about the Resurrection.

"Look, kid," Sturdley said quickly, "it probably wasn't as bad as it looked."

John's boyish face grew solemn. "Oh, no, it was bad. You can ask Peg Faber. She saw it, too. Thomas came at us. I don't know what would have happened if we hadn't, uh, managed to get away."

John looked down at the table uneasily, and Sturdley realized how the kid and Peg had made their escape. John must have opened the Rift, the mysterious gateway that had allowed the giants to reach Earth.

"Look," Sturdley said, "we can discuss the personal fallout later."

"I think John has a point," Bob Gunnar said. "We knew Thomas was a hothead. He was out there alone, unsupervised."

"I'll talk to Robert—"

"That's the whole problem." Sturdley's chief editor said with a worried look. "We have to depend on the integrity of the giants."

"They're three times our height, effectively bulletproof, and they can read minds," John said, cracking his knuckles. "And we have no control over them."

"So Thomas has an attitude problem. So what?" Sturdley said. "The fans love that in a character. Look at the sales of *Jumboy*."

"Jumboy is just ink on paper," John said quietly. "Thomas is a real person, who can hit and hurt people."

Sturdley stared around the room, taking in the suddenly thoughtful faces. "The easiest way to make Thomas toe the line is to turn the spotlight on him," he said, talking fast. "We'll make him a star. The fans will love the rough edges, and the other giants will keep an eye on him. I've been looking over the group of newcomers, and there's a cute redhead who cracks jokes.

They'll be our next projects—*The Titanic Thomas* and *The Rampaging Ruth*."

The room exploded in a torrent of suggestions and volunteers. Sturdley enjoyed the look on Burke's face as his supposed supporters fell over themselves trying to line up jobs on the potential new bestsellers.

"Don't overextend yourselves," Sturdley warned. "If we want these books to hit at the right time, they'll have to be ready by August, for the San Diego Comics Convention."

The sound level in the conference room rose further. Late in August, San Diego became the Mecca of the comics world as writers, artists, publishers, booksellers, and fans gathered for the country's largest annual comics convention. Prestigious awards were presented, deals were made, fans met their idols and bought collectibles—and the hottest new comics were announced.

But Sturdley didn't just plan to announce the new hero titles—he intended to launch them at the con.

Gunnar ran a hand back through his thinning hair, his lantern jaw tightening. "We just came off a crash schedule getting *Robert* and *Barbara* ready," he complained. "Now you're sticking me with a bare three-month lead to get two more books through production?"

"It'll be worth it," Sturdley said confidently. "All we need is a couple of seasoned, fast artists who can capture the characters. I'd ask you, Marty, but I know you're up to your butt with *Mr. Pain,* the *Glamazon* start-up, and of course, *Latter-Day Breed.*" That final Burke project had been repeatedly announced, then set back, for almost a year. It was fast becoming a legendary "never-was" in the fan world. "But maybe you can suggest some people for *Thomas* and *Ruth*. Get back to me on it as soon as you can.

"I think that's all we need to discuss for now," Sturdley called over the cross-talk in the room. The young artists were already leaving, discussing where they could find photo references of the two newly anointed comics heroes. "Has this Ruth babe got big boobs?" Grantfield was asking. "What about her hips? Is she a Grantfield babe?"

"Meeting adjourned," Sturdley cried, making the rush for the doors official. John Cameron was holding the door for Yvette Zelcerre when Sturdley came up to him. "Stick around, kid," he said in a low voice.

John stayed where he was, acting as impromptu doorman until the conference room was empty. Sturdley beckoned him over to one of the seats, but stayed on his feet, watching the door swing closed. He loomed over the seated kid.

"What the hell's the big idea?" Sturdley snarled. "I had that meeting running on an even keel, and you go opening up some unrelated can of worms to scare people about our hero titles."

"I'm not concerned about the comics," John said, then shook his head. "I never thought I'd hear myself say that, but it's true. I'm worried about those giants. Ever since Robert and Maurice pushed through when I opened the Rift . . ." He spread his hands pleadingly, looking up at Harry's face. "You didn't listen to me then. But If you had seen Thomas—"

"I don't need to see Thomas," Sturdley cut him off. "My job is comics—and I'm damned concerned about them. I keep this company going. What I don't need is some snot-nosed kid telling me how to run things—making me look bad in front of the whole staff."

He poked a stiff finger into John's chest. "Maybe you've got a short memory, but I *made* you, kid. I gave you the shot at *Robert.* And I could just as easily give it over to one of the drawing piranhas who were circling this table today. Remember that. Remember which side your bread is buttered on. And remember who the hell you owe, and who you should be supporting!"

John sat very still, his boyish face blank. Then, silently, he rose from his chair until he stood at his full height, looking slightly down at Harry.

"Mr. Sturdley," John finally said, "I told you the truth about the giants. They scare me, and I wish I'd never opened the Rift and brought them here."

His face hardened, but there was sadness in his deep blue, almost purple, eyes.

"And if *you'd* admit the truth," John said, "you'd say you were scared of them, too."

CHAPTER 3

"Hey, Peg, you look great today," Zeb Grantfield said as he sauntered up to Peg Faber's desk. There was a mechanical smile on his acne-scarred features, and his eyes were scanning her desk rather than searching out her cleavage as usual. "You wouldn't happen to have any pictures of the giants—I mean, the heroes?"

Peg had gotten this request too many times to count since yesterday's staff meeting. "Just a few shots of Robert, Maurice, and maybe Barbara," she said, not even reaching for the file drawer.

"I was thinking of maybe Thomas and Ruth," Grantfield said quickly.

Sure, Peg thought. The two new titles Harry's pushing. And like most of the would-be Michelangelos around here, Zeb can only draw from photo reference. She shrugged. "You might try Yvette Zelcerre's people first. If that doesn't work, go to the newspapers. I don't think the celebrity photo places would have any shots yet."

"Yeah." Grantfield nodded. "I already tried them." He sped off without a backward look.

Peg's eyes didn't follow him, going instead to the wooden door behind her chair, the entrance to Harry Sturdley's office. Harry never had closed-door meetings. But John Cameron had been in there for half an hour. She knew that John was pages ahead of his workload on *The Amazing Robert.* What was going on? She hoped to find out when John finally emerged.

But when John Cameron at last stepped into the corridor a few moments later, he didn't look in the mood for conversation. His wide shoulders were slumped, and there was a frown on his normally placid, boyish face as the door slammed shut behind him. He gave her a halfhearted smile.

Peg beckoned him over. "What's the matter? You look like you're carrying the weight of the world on your shoulders."

"Could you do me a favor, Peg?"

"Sure—if I can," Peg said warily.

"Could you talk to Mr. Sturdley—tell him what you . . . we . . . saw that day. What Thomas was doing." He broke off, then took a deep breath. "Look, we know the giants aren't really heroes. Now we've got to get Mr. Sturdley to understand."

"Was that what you were trying to do after the meeting yesterday? Is that why you two came out last?"

John shook his head. "I tried to do it *during* the meeting. Mr. Sturdley yelled at me. And he just yelled at me again."

She shook her head. "Oh, John." He'd probably gone about it exactly the wrong way. But she had to admire John's courage. Harry Sturdley was his hero. It must have been tough for John to tell Harry he was making a mistake.

As she opened her mouth to tell him that, Peg saw a stranger coming down the hallway to the executive suites. "Can I help you?" she asked.

The man was tall and well-built, but curiously non-descript, his face unremarkable over the sort of clothes that blend well into crowds. He's just what I always expected a real-life spy to look like, Peg thought.

"I'm here to see Mr. Sturdley," the man said in a quiet, neutral voice.

Peg frowned. There was nothing on the appointment calendar, and judging the mood he must be in after chewing out John, Harry wouldn't be receptive to unannounced callers. What were the people at front reception thinking of? "I'm afraid you've chosen a bad time. He's just finished a major meeting, and he's very busy—"

"He'll see me." The man didn't raise his voice, but there was an undercurrent of confidence—absolute assurance—that flustered Peg a little.

The man nodded toward her phone. "Just tell him it's Quentin Farley."

Even as Peg was marshaling objections, her hand moved to the intercom button. She stabbed a finger down, to have Harry Sturdley's voice crackle in her ears. "What?"

"There's a gentleman to see you. Quentin Far—"

Sturdley broke in. "Quentin Farley? Send him right in."

Peg rose to open the door for Farley, to find Harry rushing out. He shook hands with the stranger, hustled him in, then shut the door behind them.

"Weird," Peg said. "What do you think that's all about?" She turned back to John, only to find him walking away, already halfway down the hall.

"Perfect," she muttered to herself. "This is turning into a *great* day."

* * *

Harry Sturdley extended his hand toward a chair. "Sit down, Mr. Farley. Can I get you something to drink? A coffee?"

As he spoke, Sturdley stepped behind his desk, putting away sketches of Thomas and Ruth, the two stars-to-be. It seemed as if half the art staff was submitting proposals for the new books. But Sturdley pushed all that onto the back burner. This man had information he had to know. "Have you found him?"

Farley shook his head.

Harry felt a spurt of irrational anger. Ira Orreck had recommended this guy as the best detective he knew, but Farley looked like a nobody.

"It's a challenging job," Farley began quietly.

"I just want to know where Gideon is," Sturdley interrupted. "Is that so tough?"

"I can give you an educated guess," the detective said. "The odds are that he's up in the compound in Westchester, the estate the press is now calling Heroes' Manor."

"But you haven't seen him up there."

"From what my agency has been able to check on the comings and goings of the giants—"

"Heroes," Harry automatically corrected.

Farley shrugged. "We've generally pinpointed forty-seven ah, heroes at a time. Gideon seems always to be missing. But two other giants from the remaining total—usually males—also disappear." The detective leaned forward. "They seem to be gone in six-hour, rotating shifts."

"Like guards," Sturdley muttered. So, they hadn't just dragged Gideon off to drown him. That was a start.

"One could put it that way—if one had any idea

what the hell was going on." Farley's quiet eyes watched him like a hawk.

"Orreck said you were discreet," Sturdley said. "But there are things I can't tell you. I just want to make sure that Gideon is all right."

Farley sighed. "Easier said than done, Mr. Sturdley. When you established Heroes' Manor, you created an excellent security setup for them. Since the orientation period when you were teaching the heroes how to deal with our society, there has been no human live-in staff at the compound."

"I didn't want any press leaks going out about the heroes' private lives," Harry explained.

"Well, you certainly made sure of the privacy," Farley said dryly. "Especially since none of our operatives are supposed to speak with the giants—excuse me, heroes. That means our only inside intelligence has been gained by operatives disguised as delivery people."

He paused for a second, then gave Sturdley a direct look. "And those operatives found their intelligence-gathering somewhat circumscribed, since the surveillance subjects are apparently able to read minds."

"Ah . . . yes." Sturdley tugged at his collar.

"They also seemed amazingly adept at finding the listening devices—'bugs' if you will—that my agents tried to leave behind. We finally stopped attempting to place them—after one of my staff was approached in a threatening manner."

"Threatening?" Sturdley said.

"One of your heroes told him rather bluntly to get while the going was good. It seems your orientation people did an excellent job of teaching the giants colloquial speech."

"Couldn't you sneak somebody into the place?"

Sturdley asked desperately. "I mean, there are acres of woods out there. All you'd have to do is pop someone over the fence—"

"We attempted infiltration last night." Farley's quiet voice took on the slightest hint of "don't tell me how to do my job."

"And?"

"Our infiltrator had a brisk chase through the forest. Apparently, he was expected. And with a group of mind-readers on guard . . . well, I imagine they let our infiltrator go deliberately—to discourage any others. This man had special forces training—he was a recon Marine. And he considered himself lucky to get away."

"So he didn't learn anything?"

Farley gave him another direct look. "We learned that the giants' woods skills are quite impressive—potentially lethal for any intruders."

Farley cleared his throat. "In sum, we've been reduced to passive surveillance." His lips tightened. "And I'd prefer we didn't discuss how that will be achieved."

"Fine," Sturdley said. "I just hope you have some news for me soon."

Farley rose from his seat. "So," he said, "do I."

The morning sun was just beginning to burn the mist off the lake, but there were already signs of stirring in the compound known as Heroes' Manor. There were also signs of life beneath and atop the waters of the lake that bordered the property. The trout were rising to see if there were any bugs around to snack on, and a lone fisherman's boat was drifting across the silvery water.

Quentin Farley expertly cast a handmade lure, enjoying the whir of the line as he handled the rod with practiced ease.

Farley's ordinary-looking face creased in a smile under the brim of his fly-cluttered hat. Much as he relished sport fishing, he had very little time to indulge himself. The opportunity of mixing business and pleasure . . .

He forced his mind away from that thought. The fish—concentrate on the fish, Farley reminded himself. Often on a case, he had to sink himself into a character to avoid suspicion. But against subjects who could read minds, he had to *become* the character.

There was a sudden tug on his line, and he had several minutes of thinking strictly about fishing until he finally landed a good-size trout. And all the while, his boat kept drifting gently toward Heroes' Manor.

Farley lay back in the skiff, tilting his hat to shield his eyes from the sun just clearing the hills to the east. For all the world, he looked like an early-morning sportsman loafing a bit.

At least, he hoped so.

Trying to keep his mind riveted on how the freshly caught trout would taste filleted and frying over a camp fire, Farley turned his head slightly and dug a pair of binoculars from under the thwarts of the boat.

With the sun behind him to avoid reflecting light on the lenses, Farley scanned what he could see of the manor. Most of the estate was woodland, with the occasional manicured lawn and two topiary gardens filled with fanciful creatures. The area around the main buildings was cleared, of course, as was most of the lakefront. A dilapidated boathouse and pier were in easy walking distance of the main house.

One thing was quickly evident. The giants were outdoors people, apparently even sleeping al fresco. The human-size buildings would have been intolerably cramped for them. Still, the twenty-footers seemed to have adapted several modern conveniences into their routine. Running water was one. So was modern cooking equipment, although human-scale industrial sizes were mere single-serving cookware for the giants.

A cooking crew prepared what looked like a buffet being spread in the shade of a tent that had probably seen service in a circus. Other giants, lazing by the shore or swimming, made their way over to the tent to load up platters full of goodies.

They certainly ate with good appetites.

Farley lay back again, sniffing the air to see if any food smells were wafting this way. Of course not. The breeze was coming from the other side, pushing him toward the compound.

Finding a comfortable pose, Farley scanned again, this time picking up a giant with a larger than usual appetite. This guy was juggling three platters of food as he headed off into the woods.

Three platters. Heading into the woods. Farley came fully alert, focusing in on the laden giant. His heart began to pound. Gideon. Two guards.

Keep your mind on fish, he told himself, trying to throttle back his excitement. Watch where this guy goes—and you just might be able to land the big one.

CHAPTER 4

Robert lay back on the lakefront beach, ignoring the mist and the chill in the air. The protective mental aura that always surrounded the giants repelled the moisture.

At the moment, what most concerned Robert was breakfast—and the nearness of Barbara, who knelt in the sand just beyond his left shoulder. Robert was debating whether to share the favorite delicacy on his platter with his lover. It was a cylinder of yellow fruit, almost as long as his index finger, called pineapple. He'd never eaten anything like it until coming here, and he found the tart-sweet taste almost addictive.

A little research had shown him pictures of pineapples in their native state, rather like oversize pine cones. He'd also learned that they were flown in from an area known as the tropics, where the weather patterns were too warm to be believed.

Pineapple was also on the expensive side, but he had decreed that there would always be some available at least for breakfast. Robert took a bite, savoring the taste as ever, then turned lazily to offer the remainder to Barbara.

Beyond her, he saw Victor tramping off into the woods with the food platters. It was then that his mental senses caught a sudden flicker of excitement, of triumph.

Robert sat bolt upright. Someone was spying on them!

He tried to zero in on the source, cutting past the shielded, unaware hum of his companions' thoughts. Robert had become used to one thing in recent days. Just as passage through the Rift had refined the giants' mental powers, making them considerably stronger, Robert's powers were stronger still.

Perhaps it was because after escaping from his world to this one, he had passed through the Rift twice more—once to return to his homeworld, and again to lead his people here. In any case, the potency of his immaterial abilities was much increased. And he could detect thoughts much farther off and from weaker sources than any of the others.

He began to get fishing imagery, and turned his attention to the lake. Yes. There, out in the middle of the water, was a boat with a watcher. Gathering his mental energies, Robert shot a probe across the lake, right into the brain of the spy. He read the disorientation, the fear his powerful intrusion caused.

It was an unequal struggle, Robert's brute-force trespass against the weak shields Lessers' minds could generate. He was through the defenses with ease, raping this Lesser named Farley of all his memories about Robert and his kind.

So *this* was the one behind the other spies with their prying, their little machines, the airplane that had tried to eavesdrop on them. And behind him was another figure, an employer . . .

Robert pushed a little harder, tearing through the last defenses.

And he saw the face of Harry Sturdley.

Surprise made Robert pull back slightly, and the terrified mind he'd been rummaging in tore itself free.

Cursing, Robert leapt to his feet and flung himself toward the lake. Two giant strides, and he dove in, cutting through the water like a great beast. But ahead of him, he heard the snarl of an outboard motor coming to life. Robert swam on, aiming for the terror emanating from Farley's mind. In the end, however, even he had to admit that a Master's muscles could not compete against the Lessers' powerful little machines.

He turned back with a snarl as Farley's thoughts receded. Coming back to the shore, he saw two figures standing on the beach, staring out at him.

"What were you doing?" Barbara asked as he rose dripping from the water. Standing behind her, giving him a quizzical look, was Thomas, running a hand through his sandy hair.

"I was chasing a spy," Robert said bluntly. "He was out in a boat on the water, watching us through the long-distance glasses the Lessers use. I think he saw Victor bringing the meals to Gideon and the guards."

Thomas' hands bunched into fists. "And he got away?"

Robert nodded. "But I know who he was working for. *Sturdley*."

"I warned you that little man would make trouble," Barbara said. "The nerve to spy on us! He needs to learn proper respect."

"I'll grind him like a bug," Thomas rumbled.

Robert abruptly shook his head. "No. We still need Sturdley, his money, and the prestige he's providing for us."

"We can't afford to let this go," Barbara warned.

"I don't intend to." Robert told her, his voice cold. "We also can't afford to kill him just yet. But there are other ways to bring Harry Sturdley to heel. So far, we have led him on through greed."

He ran his fingers through his wet hair, pushing it back. "Now we'll show how it is to be led through fear. I've already chosen the target. His death will not only send a message to Sturdley, but also further our plans for this world."

"Who is it?" Barbara asked.

A slow smile crept over Robert's face. "John Cameron."

"The one who brought us here?" Thomas said.

"The one uncontrollable element on this world," Robert corrected him. "The Lessers, despite their machines and weapons, we can manipulate and, finally, dominate. But Cameron—he doesn't fit into the scheme of things. I know for a fact that he has raised mental shields against detection. Who knows what other powers he has? He's an unknown factor, who might conceivably prove a match for us."

"There are many of us, and only one of him," Thomas pointed out.

"We can't follow if he flees through the Rift." Robert shook his head decisively. "I want this world safe for us, with no unguardable doors to other universes." His eyes were like stone as he glared at the other two giants. "What if he opened the way for some of our old rivals from home?"

Barbara and Thomas stood very still, digesting that suggestion. Unease showed on Thomas' face. Barbara's lovely features radiated sheer animal fear.

"How, then, should we deal with him?" Barbara asked, her voice tense.

Robert smiled, showing his Mastery over them. "We must seem to do nothing. The Lessers cannot see us dirty our hands. Although Sturdley will know."

"Then how . . .?" Thomas began in bafflement.

"When one does not wish to dirty one's hands, one uses a tool," Robert said coolly. "Barbara, make my costume ready. I must go into the city."

Clad in the skintight white attire of the heroes, Robert spent a cramped hour getting down to Manhattan. The southbound highways were filled with commuter traffic, and the vehicle that carried the leader of the giants had been built more for space than comfort.

Robert rode in the back of a moving van, thanks to yet another licensing ploy of Harry Sturdley's. A national van line had paid sizably for the opportunity to paint several old trucks white and designate them heromobiles.

The trailer was not tall enough to allow Robert to stand erect, but he could sit upright and curse the lack of cushioning material. That would, he was assured, be forthcoming, as well as panels in the ceiling to allow for illumination.

As it was, however, he bumped along in the darkness for what felt like altogether too long, making mental memos to himself. Item: arrange for transport that does not depend on the Lessers. That could be arranged later when Sturdley was more firmly under their thumb.

It took Robert the better part of the day to find the man he sought—the tool he'd decided to use.

The street gang playing basketball in the downtown playground suddenly felt the shadow looming over them. Dwayne-O was going for the layup, when a huge hand suddenly blocked him, plucking the ball away.

"Damn!" the kid burst out as he fell to the ground empty-handed. He glared up ready to attack the interloper, then grinned. "Damn, white boy, you wanna play, you can be on my team!"

"Tell me what I want to know," Robert said. He hefted the foot-wide basketball in his palm as if it were a child's toy. "I'm looking for a man. Frederick Hardiman."

"Don't know nobody—" Dwayne-O instantly began.

Robert cut him off. "On the street, he's known as Blood."

The gang members glanced at one another for a fleeting instant, then Dwayne-O spoke again. "I *said,* we don't know nobody by that name."

"So let us get on with our b'ball and screw off," one of the others said, solidarity generating bravado.

Robert didn't return the ball. He kept it in his palm, pressing his fingers into it, distorting the sphere until it finally ruptured with a violent *bang*!

The players stared up at him in fear and silence.

"I wonder," Robert said in a mediative voice, "how it would feel to do that with a head?"

It abruptly turned out that there was someone known as Blood playing ball two courts over.

Unfortunately, that person wasn't the Blood whom Robert was seeking. And, as he discovered through the day, Blood was a very popular name in the streets. He encountered a pimp, two loan-sharks, several illegal pharmaceutical salesmen, and five strong-arm thugs who all rejoiced in that sobriquet.

It was nearly sunset before Robert found the Blood whose real name was Frederick Hardiman. He'd gotten his first clue after he'd cleared out a Harlem bar. Pursuing that had involved breaking up an armed robbery where one of the criminals had been unwise enough to shoot at him. Guns were becoming rare in New York after the heroes had set up a de facto blockade, intercepting illegal weapons being smuggled in from down south.

That, after all, had been how Robert first met Frederick Hardiman, a.k.a. Blood. A courier for the king of the arms dealers, Blood had been driving the first vanload of weapons the heroes had ever stopped.

Now guns were old business for Robert. The bullets were stopped by his protective aura. Then he merely twisted the gun away and crushed it in one hand. As a personal lesson, Robert also broke the gunman's right arm.

The gunman's partner in crime was the one Robert wanted. And he talked loud and long after seeing Robert in action. Armed with the information he got there, Robert set off for an address in the far west Forties.

Blood felt a deep sense of injustice against the world. This was a comedown, and he knew it. Two months ago, he'd been a trusted courier, delivering thousands of dollars worth of arms from the southern states. Now he was just a common leg-breaker, working for chump change.

He shifted his grip on the baseball bat in his hand, lining up another swing as his associate held the customer—a deadbeat debtor—upright. Blood scowled in pain. His shoulder still hadn't healed from his fateful run-in with that big freak of a giant. Blood lined up for a knee-cracking shot when his partner glanced down toward the mouth of the alley, went pale, and ran. The guy they were beating sagged to the filth-covered ground.

Blood glanced over his shoulder, rolled his eyes and threw the bat away. *"Man!"* he said in disgust. "Can't do *nothin'* anymore without some big white bastid stickin' his nose in!"

Robert strolled down the alleyway, ignoring the unconscious form on the ground and the thug vaulting over a back fence. He stood over Blood. "I want to talk to you," Robert said.

Blood looked up at those familiar, perfect features. "Why the hell should I want to talk to you?" he demanded. "Last time I saw you, you got cops all over me, my boss had to put up bail, and your friend screwed up my shoulder."

"It's your boss I really want to talk to," Robert told the thug. "Maybe he and I can do some business."

"Too late to do business with him," Blood told the giant. "You blew his whole operation. He pissed at you, man. Don't expect no favors—urk!"

Robert had grown tired of the verbal sparring. He seized hold of the front of Blood's shirt and yanked him forward. This one's mind was far less organized than the spy's. It was easier to smash through the defenses, but then he was forced to grub around in Blood's memories, dredging up the information he needed. There was the boss' name, Antony Carron. Here was a mental image. Excellent. There was a considerable amount of unpleasant material to be waded through as well, and for a moment, Robert considered simply ending this Lesser. But no. He was a necessary conduit. And there were some useful subconscious memories—items that Blood didn't even know he knew.

Robert plundered what he wanted, then pulled back to confront Blood eye-to-eye rather than mind-to-mind. The thug swayed back and forth on his feet, and a sharp stink told Robert that the little man had lost control of his bladder.

"Wha . . . Wha'd you do?" Blood asked woozily.

"I got the information I wanted," Robert told him. "And now I have a job for you. I want you to go and see Mr. Antony Carron. I have a proposition—what do you call it? A *contract* I want to offer him."

"Why him?" Blood's voice was raw, almost a scream. "Why *me*?"

"Mr. Carron has shown himself to be a clever man," Robert said. "I want to use that cleverness."

He stared down at the soiled figure that had once been a tough, confident street thug as if he were looking at a loathsome form of insect life. "As for you, you'll do what I ask. Unless you want to see how it feels to have your limbs plucked off—one at a time."

CHAPTER 5

A scowl darkened Joey Santangelo's broken-nosed face as he opened the door of the north Jersey estate. "What the hell you doing here, Blood?" he asked. His left hand remained on the handle of the thick redwood door. His right gripped a heavy assault rifle. "I hope you ain't here for money," Joey warned. "The boss ain't shelling out the way he did in the good old days."

Blood shook his head. "I got a message," he said. "It's business." Since speaking with Robert, he'd cleaned up and rented the car, but he was still gray with shock from his psychic rape. Several times along the drive he'd had to pull to the side of the road when his hands started shaking uncontrollably. It was a little past dawn when he arrived in north Jersey.

Unlike most crime bosses, however, Antony Carron was already awake. He gestured slightly with a slim, deeply tanned hand, indicating a seat for Blood to take, his hooded eyes not leaving the early morning news program on his projection-system TV. A commercial came on, and Carron killed the image with a tap on a remote control, turning as Blood began his report. Perfect teeth glistened in a shark's smile as he heard the gist of Robert's offer. "So, the giants need someone out of the way, and they're willing to pay big to get the job done."

Carron had to laugh at the irony. The people who had chased him out of New York for gun running were now prepared to hire him—for a hit.

"There are conditions," Blood said. "First, they want it done outside of town."

"Away from their territory," Carron said, nodding. "Of course. They don't want any blood spattering their pretty white uniforms. Yes. That makes sense."

Carron started to laugh again. Then he turned to his main minion, savoring the humor of it all. "What do you think, Joey? We'll be taking comic-book money to waste a cartoonist."

Carron's aquiline features showed a little disappointment when Santangelo didn't get the joke. But it really didn't matter. Right now, Carron could use the money. And he could appreciate the humor in accepting a hit from a group most of the media was heralding as saviors of society. Business as usual, he thought. The cleanest-looking civic and industrial leaders were usually the ones with the dirtiest business to be done.

Besides, it wouldn't hurt to have a major marker to call in from the magnetic, oh-so-idolized leader of the giants. Carron revolved plans for contacts and payment in his head. He and Robert would never meet. The rest of the negotiations would take place through a series of cut-outs, both for the sake of the giant's reputation—and just in case this turned out to be some kind of incredible sting operation.

Carron knew it wasn't a setup, though. Ever since he was young, he could feel murder in his bones. For some reason, these king-size freaks needed John Cameron out of their way—and they were willing to pay big for it.

Weeks later, after the terms of the deal had been arranged, Antony Carron took his Porsche out for a spin. The powerful machine needed considerable control on the curves of the country road, or it would wind up crashing into some of the pretty greenery. Carron frowned when his car phone began to bleat. He picked up the receiver and answered with a simple "Yes?"

The good thing about cellulars was that they couldn't be traced. The drawback was that conversations were carried on over the air, where anybody could monitor them.

A deep, rumbling voice was on the other end of the staticy circuit. "This is Robert," the voice announced.

Carron was so surprised, he almost swerved off the road and into a tree. A second or two later, he managed to pull onto a grassy margin. "I didn't think we'd be dealing personally," he said in a neutral voice. Contempt twisted his fine features. The giant had revealed himself to be an amateur.

"I merely wanted to expedite matters," Robert responded, "to get this news to you as quickly as possible. Your . . . target will be out of town in August."

Carron nodded at his unseen listener. At least the giant had the sense not to mention names over the air. "Where?"

"There's a convention in California. A comics convention, in a place called San Diego."

A mirthless smile tugged at Carron's lips. "Such a dangerous place, the West Coast. One always hears about drive-by killings and the like."

"Yes," Robert agreed, "one does."

"I thank you for the information." Antony Carron was about to hang up when something else struck him. He stared at his car phone. "None of our contacts know this number," he suddenly said. "How did *you* get it?"

Miles away, Robert smiled into a custom-made, giant-size cellular phone. The number had been easy. It was an unconscious memory he had pillaged from Blood's mind—a mental picture of the interior of Carron's car with the phone and its number. But Robert was not about to tell the crime lord how he'd gotten it.

"Consider it a sample of our abilities," he told Carron, "and a reminder not to underestimate us."

Peg Faber stepped out of the elevator onto the floor that housed the Fantasy Factory offices. She had two reasons to feel guilty as she slunk down the hallway. For one thing, she was coming back from lunch rather late. For another, she'd spent that lunch with an old boyfriend.

She had gone out with Lew Irvine in college. He'd been a senior, she a freshman. In the time since they'd broken up, he'd breezed through law school and was now an associate at a prestigious firm. How appropriate that he'd become a lawyer, Peg thought. He was always so persuasive . . .

Her heart-shaped face reddened. At least he was always persuading me to do things I wouldn't normally have done.

Obviously that eloquent streak still held. Lew had caught sight of her during the media hoopla over the giants, and had called the Fantasy Factory to see if the redhead on the screen was the Peg Faber he remembered. That phone reunion had led inevitably to drinks, and then Peg hadn't been able to refuse a lunch date.

For the last couple of weeks, the Fantasy Factory had been like a pressure cooker gathering steam. Preparations for the San Diego convention had proceeded apace, and Peg had found herself getting swamped with the details. She'd handled preparations for other cons in her first year at the office, but this was the biggie. In addition to juggling flights, room assignments, and filling spots for the panels on the program, she'd also had to deal with incredible in-house politicking as artists and editors plotted and schemed to get tickets to the West Coast.

If all the staffers had gotten their way, the offices would have been empty for the week before the con—everyone would have set off early for a vacation in the sun. That wasn't going to happen with the amount of work to be done—especially with the final preparations for the launch of *The Titanic Thomas* and *The Rampaging Ruth.*

Everybody had a full plate—and in Peg's case, there were several courses to go. Today was not the day to have been talked into a long lunch.

Peg was still twenty feet from her desk when she spotted Harry Sturdley standing in his doorway, doing a slow burn.

"How nice of you at last to grace us with your presence," he said with heavy sarcasm as she scampered the final distance. "Perhaps you hadn't noticed, but this is an office, and work is not supposed to be an optional activity. Assistants, oddly enough, are supposed to *assist* people. Where's the file on movie offers for the heroes?"

"R-right here," Peg said through a suddenly tight throat. She leaned over her desk, her mop of red curls hiding a face equally red.

"Hey, Peg." John Cameron came strolling down the

hall, an artist's portfolio tucked under his arm. "I didn't catch you before—"

"That's because she's been out at lunch for the past two hours," Sturdley said caustically. "I'm afraid she's exceeded her goof-off quota for today. So unless this is business—buzz off."

Peg didn't meet John's eyes, but she saw him back off a step at Harry's tirade. "Hey, Mr. Sturdley, lighten up a little."

Peg glanced through the curtain of her hair to find John looking at her with concern. "If Peg was a little late today, lots of times she's only taken a sandwich at her desk to cover things for you."

"Yeah, well she didn't do that today," Sturdley growled. "And she should know better with the schedule we're running under."

Harry Sturdley was in a bad mood. For the last half hour, he'd been on the phone with Quentin Farley, getting an update on the surveillance of Heroes' Manor. The detective had almost quit the job some weeks before, and insisted that if the surveillance was to continue, it would be done by high-power telescopes from the other side of the lake. Farley had refused to explain why he wanted things that way, but he hinted it was for the safety of his operatives. Obviously *something* had happened to make the investigator mighty leery of close-up work around the giants.

Sturdley's annoyance was fueled by the fact that he still had nothing to show for the money he was shelling out to have the place watched. Oh, he had piles of grainy photographs shot through telephoto lenses, and reports of meals being brought into the forest—*three* meals. But Gideon was still gone, and pairs of heroes kept dropping out of sight in regular rotation.

It all seemed to point to Gideon's being held prisoner someplace in the woods. But Farley and his fellow detectives hadn't been able to get their hands on *proof.* If they could come up with a picture of Gideon, or even a sighting, that would give Harry some clout in a showdown with Robert.

Harry Sturdley had never been afraid to mix it up in an argument. But when it came to the subject of Robert and Gideon, for the first time in his life, Harry kept backing away from a confrontation.

This was not a fight to stroll into with empty hands. No way was Harry going up against somebody more than three times his size without solid evidence of wrongdoing. Not while there was so much to be done in preparation for San Diego. He'd talk to Farley again, after the convention. Maybe by then the investigators would have something he could use. If not, then he'd try tackling Robert. It was better to wait.

Coward, a little voice jeered from the depths of his aching head. While Peg had been off on her long lunch date, he hadn't touched a bite. Acid roiled in Sturdley's stomach, sending sour fumes up to burn the back of his throat.

Maybe he was taking out his frustrations on Peg. Too bad. That was part of the job. And no snotty-nosed kid was going to tell him how to operate his office.

John Cameron's open, boyish face tightened a little under Harry's continuing glare. But he held his ground.

"What's the problem, kid? You dreaming again?" Harry's voice seemed to grate in his chest. "I told you to buzz off."

"I can't believe Happy Harry Sturdley would treat people like this. I'm sorry if you're having a bad day—"

"The art for the next *Robert* book is almost due,"

Sturdley interrupted, switching to a new attack. "Why don't you get to work on that instead of hanging around here? Or rather, hanging around *her?*"

They both glanced to where a miserably embarrassed Peg kept her eyes on her desk, pretending to go through files.

John's face tightened still further. "If you think you've got a problem with me, yell away. But let's keep it with me. You want to know where the art for the next *Robert* issue is? I just had it copied."

Sturdley gazed at him wordlessly, feeling a little foolish.

John misread the silence, taking it for doubt. He yanked at the zipper on his portfolio, resting it on the edge of Peg's desk, then drew out a sheaf of illustration boards. Yes, here was the latest *Robert* story, drawn and inked in John's unique, exquisite style—and ahead of schedule.

"Well? Don't you want to check it?" John stepped forward, rattling the boards. The portfolio tipped, and its contents scattered over the top of Peg's desk. With a wordless cry, she began gathering up the debris.

"Hold on a second," Sturdley suddenly said, looking over her shoulder. His eyes were riveted on a sketchpad Peg had just picked up.

It was covered with quickly done marker studies, more impressionistic than John Cameron's usual work. But even in rough outline, the cityscapes on the paper were breathtaking.

It wasn't New York, or any other city Sturdley had ever seen, but the high-flung towers caught his interest immediately. They were futuristic buildings, with a soaring architecture that would have driven Hugh Ferris or Alex Raymond mad with envy. Harry wasn't sure of the scale, but the city seemed to stretch to the horizon and literally scraped the sky. And those dots in the sky . . . they were awfully sketchy, but the nearer ones had enough detail to indicate arms and legs.

They were human figures—flying through the sky.

"What's this?" Sturdley asked, taking the pad from Peg and riffling through the pages.

"Doodles," John said quickly. "Just something I've been fooling around with."

Sturdley frowned, staring from sketch to sketch. Something about the work bothered him. Then his practiced eye finally caught it. The city had been drawn from several different perspectives, but the center of the composition remained constant—not as if John were trying a new arrangement, *but as if he were drawing the scene from life.*

Harry Sturdley turned to the young artist. "This is a real place, isn't it?" he asked. "Someplace else you've visited, where people fly."

John suddenly snatched the sketchpad out of Sturdley's hand, then gathered the rest of his stuff from Peg. All he left on her desk was the pile of illustration boards for *The Amazing Robert.*

Thumping his fist on the artwork, he said loudly, "There's the *Robert* stuff. That's our business—Right?" Then John clamped the portfolio under his arm. "What's in here—that's *my* business!"

He turned on his heel and stormed down the corridor.

Harry and Peg both looked at each other in silence. Everyone knew that on bad days Happy Harry sometimes went on a rampage.

But they had never, *ever* seen John Cameron angry before.

CHAPTER 6

Warm breath tickled Marty Burke's ear as Leslie Ann Nasotrudere sighed, then made contented crooning sounds. She lay atop him, eyelids fluttering, her body soft and warm, their flesh plastered together by the thin film of sweat from their lovemaking. As ever, he couldn't get over the change from her TV persona: the tight, tense, alert—Peg Faber had once described her as plastic—newswoman, and the armful of female he held now. In the warm tent of the tangled bedclothes, Leslie Ann was tender, even vulnerable.

Sharp teeth nipped his earlobe. "Whatcha thinking?" Leslie Ann asked.

Burke grinned, running his hands over the supple curve of her back. "I was wondering if we had time for one more tussle before we headed back to our offices."

"Horny devil," she reproved him.

"Hey, I've got lots of time for nooners," Burke said bitterly. "It's not like I'm an artist for the *heroes*."

Leslie Ann slid her model's body across his. The mattress of the hotel bed shifted as she rose up beside him, fluffing her short blond hair. She looked down at Burke, her eyes thoughtful. "My producer has told me to lay off the big guys. Official policy right now at I.N.C. is pretty pro-hero. And as their newest newscaster, I don't carry much clout. I still think people will turn against those overgrown freaks," she said frankly. "But it won't be for a while yet."

Leslie Ann's face hardened a little. "I may have to lay off the heroes, but the brass didn't say anything about Sturdley. I think I've figured out a way to get at him—I'll expose him as an exploiter."

"He sure as hell is!" Burke said, sitting up to face her. "For years, he's grabbed the glory while the real talents were supposed to stay quietly at their drawing boards. Mention the Fantasy Factory, and most people will know of Harry Sturdley. But what about guys like Reece Yantsey, or Kyle Everard . . ." He thumped a hand to his bare chest. "Or me?"

She shook her head, her newscaster's mask firmly in place. "Get real, Burke. Out in the world, who cares about a bunch of comic-book artists, for chrissakes?"

"Then who is Sturdley exploiting?" Burke asked in bafflement.

"Who does the public love—according to the latest INC/Gallup poll?" Leslie Ann asked, her voice silky.

"Well, you were just saying that the heroes—"

She nodded. "Those good-hearted—no, make that *big*-hearted visitors from another world who are working to make our city—even better, our *planet*—a safer place. They go on patrol, risking life and limb—"

"They *are* bulletproof," Burke put in.

Leslie Ann made an impatient gesture. "We can use footage of the dark-haired one—Maurice—after he fell off that building and broke his arm." Her eyes glittered as she crossed her arms over her high, firm breasts. "They go through the danger, but who rakes in all the rewards? Harry Sturdley."

"Leslie Ann, the first issues of the *Robert* and *Bar-*

bara comics are getting reprinted up the wazoo," Burke said. "The giants will get big bucks in royalties."

"A measly percentage, you mean," the newswoman immediately corrected him. "Who gets the lion's share?" Perfect rosebud lips opened to reveal sharp, little teeth. "I'll show 'em. I can be pro-hero as hell, and still screw that sonofabitch—for abusing the trust of the heroes."

Kicking aside the covers, Leslie Ann headed for the bathroom. "A quick shower, then I'm off to the office," she said. "I want to start working on this angle right away."

She glanced over her shoulder. "You could help, you know. Talk to the giants. See if you can get some dirt." She continued on, but her walk turned into a sensuous strut. "You could also scrub my back in the shower."

Burke emerged from the midtown hotel with a bemused look on his face. What had he let himself get talked into? Undercover work with Leslie Ann Nasotrudere was . . . enjoyable. But undercover work *for* her—that could be dangerous.

On the other hand, she was offering the resources of a network news organization to boost the heroes. That had to translate into still better sales for their comics. As the man who intended to take over the Fantasy Factory, he'd have to keep an eye on the bottom line. And unlike Sturdley, he'd make the heroes work for the whole company. When he took over, he'd get rid of that stupid "reality only" clause from the license agreement. That way, the heroes could mix it up with the rest of the Fantasy Factory galaxy. He could see it now—Robert *versus* Meglomanic . . . or even better

Thomas against Jumboy—the battle of the bad-attitude boys.

He was dreaming of a team-up between Barbara, Ruth, and the Ex-Wives, the company's premier all-female supergroup, when he spotted a tall blond figure blocks ahead. A *very* tall blond figure—Robert, on patrol.

It was amazing to see how quickly New Yorkers had accustomed themselves to the giants. The lunch-hour crowd, always in this area at noontime, parted around Robert in the most blasé manner imaginable. Only a few tourists stopped to gawk and take pictures.

An out-of-towner screeched his car to a halt for a better look, almost causing a traffic accident. Robert shook a reproving finger, telling the motorist to drive on.

By that time, Burke had reached the giant. "Excuse me," he called up. "I'm Marty Burke, one of the artists from the Fantasy Factory. I thought it would be a good idea if we met."

Robert's blue eyes glanced down—piercing blue eyes that seemed to reach right into Burke's soul.

This little man was sleeping with one of Sturdley's enemies. He was consumed with envy for Sturdley and had his own preposterous plans for the comic-book company. What in the name of the gods below was a *Jumboy*?

Nonetheless, a rival working against Sturdley—one with a faction of supporters—could be useful. This Burke was worth cultivating.

"Marty Burke," Robert said aloud. "Of course. I very much enjoy your work on"—a delicate probe of thought winked out—*"Mr. Pain."*

"You know my work?" Burke ran a hand through his

thinning hair and his trademark ponytail. "I'm very impressed."

"Indeed," Robert said gravely, continuing his probes. "I always thought it would be fun to do a crossover."

He smiled down at the flushed face below him. This was almost too easy. He turned the conversation to the San Diego convention. Perhaps Burke knew the travel arrangements . . .

Up in the skybox of the San Diego Civic Center, Harry Sturdley stared down at a sprawling concourse of booths and moving bodies—the comics convention. The Civic Center was built in the latest style for convention spaces, a la the Crystal Palace. It looked like a giant mutated greenhouse, with a few concrete buttresses to break up the smoked glass.

Not that anyone on the convention floor was looking up. The eyes of the convention-goers seemed glued to the wares spread out on the tables of the comics dealers—comics, graphic novels, toys, books, videotapes. Those who weren't buying were clustering around the booths of the various comics companies, meeting the artists and writers of their favorite books. Even now, early in the con, long lines were forming for autographs.

Harry shook his head. The crowd seemed substantially larger than last year's record-breaking attendance. Thousands of people streamed between the two gigantic statues of robots that marked the entrance to the convention floor. The press of bodies dangerously crammed the aisles between tables and booths. He said as much to the young woman at the control panel.

"Don't worry, Mr. Sturdley," she reassured him, "we

can take any crowd-control measures necessary from up here."

"That's incredible." He turned to get a better look at the panel. One readout was labeled CROWD DENSITY. It was a simple vernier dial, a needle going across a scale, but still well short of the red zone marked OVERCROWDED.

As Sturdley leaned over, he rested one hand on the panel. Suddenly, klaxons were screaming an alarm. The young woman twisted in her chair. "What did you do?"

Harry looked over at his hand in embarrassment. "I must have brushed that control," he said, pointing to an unmarked black switch in the upper right corner.

"Ohmigod!" the young woman cried, grabbing to turn the thing off. An electric *crackle* ran through the board, then a sizzling sound as the woman screamed, jerking spastically over the panel as sparks flew wildly. She managed to tear herself free, but fell to the floor, still twitching.

The entire control panel was now dead.

Then Harry heard the screams from below. He stared out the windows of the skybox and drew a hoarse breath—the two statues at the entrance were moving. Both of the twenty-foot-tall robots were lifting their feet—and bringing them down on the trembling crowd members waiting to get in. People were running in terror as the enormous feet went up and came down, as if the robots were crushing grapes. But it wasn't wine that spread in a dark-red stain across the convention floor.

One of the titanic figures pivoted and looked up at Sturdley, waving an arm. Its other hand removed a metallic mask, revealing the face of Robert. "Don't worry,

Harry," the giant's voice rumbled across the shrieks and groans on the floor below. "We'll control this crowd, even if we have to kill them all."

The entire convention center began to shake. The panes in the ceiling began to shatter, dropping shards of glass onto the milling crowd. The skybox tilted madly, and Sturdley was flung into the plate-glass window. It erupted into pieces around him, and he tumbled helplessly toward the floor forty feet below. He screamed . . .

Harry Sturdley sat bolt upright in bed, his heart jackhammering in his chest. A quiver of reaction went through his limbs as he realized it had all been a dream.

Hope I didn't disturb Myra, he thought, turning to his left. But instead of the sleeping figure of his wife, he saw only the empty half of a strange bed. Sturdley glanced around bleary-eyed as he slowly recollected where he was. This was the big suite at the San Diego Marriott. He'd flown in ahead of the other Fantasy Factory staffers to get a jump on the arrangements and to acclimatize himself. This was supposed to be the night he could take it easy.

He raised a trembling hand to his sweat-dampened forehead.

I should have known better than to eat that airline food—especially on a flight that offered Welsh Rarebit for lunch.

Peg Faber put down her purse and shuffled the papers on her desk into a new arrangement. After weeks of frantic activity, the sensation of having nothing to do felt downright foreign. For the next six days, all the big shots and quite a few medium-size shots would be out of the office, at the convention in San Diego. For the stay-at-homes, it would be more like a five-day weekend.

As Harry Sturdley's assistant, was Peg expected to play hall monitor, or could she play hooky herself? It would be nice to cut out early on Friday. Maybe she could go to the beach, catch some rays . . .

Peg glanced up as she heard someone coming down the hall. Her gray eyes went wide with dismay as she saw John Cameron strolling toward her desk.

"What are you doing *here*?" she demanded, jumping to her feet. "Your plane is taking off in less than an hour. I should know, I made your reservation. You'll never get out to the airport in time—"

Wordlessly, with just a quick look around the empty corridor, John grabbed her hand and closed his eyes in concentration.

The ground seemed to drop from under Peg's feet. They were going into the Rift! A chill ran through her body, and she instinctively closed her eyes as they plunged through unending emptiness.

Peg clung convulsively to John's hand until she felt solid ground under her again. And she felt something else—brilliant sunlight striking her closed eyes like a physical blow.

Blinking against the glare, Peg glanced around. They were in a vine-shrouded arcade, with bright sunshine angling in. She could hear the roar of surf from far below, and a cool breeze puffed into her face.

Then she focused on the sun. It was midmorning back in New York. But here, wherever that might be, the sun was barely above the horizon.

Removing her hand from John's, she stepped out into a beautiful garden, then turned to the building rising behind her, a fantasy castle in pink stucco. "What the hell is this place?" she demanded.

"It's a hotel in La Jolla," John said.

Peg's mouth dropped open. "You mean La Jolla as in California?"

John nodded vigorously. "After all your work, it didn't seem fair that you couldn't go . . . and I wanted you to . . . anyway, I talked to Elvio, and he said this was a romantic . . . I mean, a nice place, and it's close enough to San Diego, especially if you don't have to drive . . ." As the words tumbled out, John's face got redder and redder.

Peg could feel a flush rising in her own cheeks. "You wanted me to come along to the convention? That's sweet!"

"Yeah, well, I wanted somebody to be rooting for me on this dopey panel I'm on." John still sounded uncomfortable.

"Well, it's lovely. Do we have reservations?"

"Reservations?" John asked as he trailed behind her into an elegantly appointed lobby.

The desk clerk's eyebrows rose when the young couple appeared in front of him with no luggage and a request for a room. His eyebrows rose further when the pretty redhead insisted on *two* rooms. That didn't exactly fit the profile.

"We do have two vacant singles," he said, consulting his listings. "If you'll just give me your credit card, I'll take an imprint—"

"Credit card?" John sounded even more abashed and somewhat hoarse.

Peg knew why. He had no credit, and no credit history. As best she'd been able to check through the public record, John Cameron hadn't existed on paper until he'd applied for a job at the Fantasy Factory a bit less than two years ago.

She began to giggle. It had been a splendid spontaneous gesture, with no preparation at all. "Don't worry," she said, digging into her purse. "I've got a Fantasy Factory corporate charge."

We should be able to afford two rooms here, she thought, if we cancel John's reservation at the Marriott and get the money back on his air fare.

"You know, this *is* a very romantic place," she whispered to John as they set off upstairs with their room keys. "But we're going to need some clothes."

"Uhm," John said, his ears going pink.

"Wanna buy them here, or Rift back and pack a bag?"

Antony Carron stood in the departure lounge at La Guardia airport, flexing his fingers into a fist.

"Where *is* he?" The words came out in a hiss of frustration. The plane to the coast would be taking off in minutes, and John Cameron still hadn't turned up at preflight registration.

After the giant had passed along the details of John Cameron's flight and itinerary at San Diego, the crime boss had swung into action immediately, aiming to take his target out on the airplane. What better place to hide a dead body—and the motives for killing it—than among a couple of hundred others?

The raw materials for a bomb were on hand already, and Carron had created a beauty. The timer was elegantly concealed as a calculator that would work and thus pass inspection. Among its circuits was a small detonation charge that would set off the plastique hidden in the lining of a carry-on bag.

He had hired a young woman who made her living as a mule—a drug carrier—to fly with the bag. She was under the impression that the lining was stuffed with a rather exotic white powder and would doubtless get a big surprise when the bag went up. There'd be no embarrassing witnesses to discuss Carron's involvement.

Dolores and the bag had breezed through the security check and gone aboard the plane at the first call for passengers.

Then John Cameron hadn't turned up.

Joey Santangelo had called twice to make sure Cameron hadn't gotten aboard unnoticed somehow. And now for the third time, they heard the announcement system paging passenger John Cameron.

It seemed that their target wasn't even in the airport. Carron pressed his right fist into the palm of his left hand, cracking his knuckles. That was a bad habit from his youth, one he never indulged anymore—unless he was completely wired.

"He's on the passenger list," Joey Santangelo repeated hopefully.

"Yes, but he's not on the goddam plane."

The absolute last call for passengers was going out over the public address system.

Carron came to a decision.

"Get Dolores off that plane and make sure the package comes out with her. We'll take it out to the car, disarm it, then come back in here."

"For what?" Joey-boy asked.

He quickly turned away and shut up at the blaze in the eyes of his boss.

"We're getting tickets on the next flight," Carron

said. "You, me, all the boys. If we can't hit him clean—while he's in the air—all right, then."

Carron's face was taut with fury. "We'll get him on the ground, down and dirty."

CHAPTER 7

Harry Sturdley felt a rush of irrational relief as he looked toward the entrance of the San Diego Civic Center and found no giant robot guardians.

The previous evening, the room had been empty and echoing with the muted susurrus of workmen laying carpet and assembling booths. Now it was filled with cacophony and wall-to-wall people as fans and collectors streamed down the aisles in search of books, autographs, and heaven knew what else. A fan who looked old enough to know better came running past, flapping a blue cape with a big orange Z on it. "Zenith lives!" the guy yelled.

Harry grinned.

"Sturdley," a dry, papery voice wheezed from behind him. Harry turned to see a dessicated little man who barely came up to his shoulder, emerging from the elevator. The man's wispy white hair was clipped in a severe brush-cut, and he wore a thousand-dollar suit over his skeletal frame.

The scary thing was that Dirk Colby had looked this way ever since he'd taken over Dynasty Comics from his father, decades ago. Colby's thin lips were twisted in a smile, and his eyes flickered lizardlike over blue-gray pouches of flesh, watching the Zenith fan run past. "You may have the bigger market share, Sturdley, but our characters still have the fans' hearts."

"I'd hate having to tell my stockholders something like that," Sturdley said. "And the way you keep 'up-dating' your characters by killing them off—"

"We just have different way of doing things, Studley." With a cold stare, Colby stalked off.

You can't make comics with smoke and mirrors, Sturdley thought, watching his skeletal rival move off into the crowd. There's got to be a little heart to them. As Colby headed down the aisle, a fan in a loud Hawaiian shirt tried to talk to him. Colby brushed the guy off without even stopping.

Problem is, that guy has no heart at all.

"Uh, Mr. Sturdley?"

Sturdley braced himself. One of the drawbacks to the big conventions was the name tags. They marked you as a pro, but some of the fans read that as *target.*

But that's one of the reasons you're here, Harry told himself—to talk to the fans.

He turned, summoning up a smile, and found himself facing John Cameron.

"You're here early, aren't you, kid? I thought your flight wasn't supposed to arrive until—"

"We came early," John said, glancing around. "Rift express."

"Oh." Sturdley nodded to show he understood. Then he stiffened. "*We*? I thought we were trying to keep this quiet, not give demonstrations. What's the use of whispering if you're going to—"

"Peg already knows, so I didn't think it would be a problem." John's shoulders hunched a little. "She worked so hard getting everything ready, I thought it would be nice for her."

"You did, huh?" Sturdley growled. Then he jammed his hands into his pockets and sighed. "You're right, you know. I should have offered Peg the opportunity. Guess I've been a little too distracted lately."

John brightened immediately. "You mean it's okay?"

"Sure. We'll have to alert the office, make up some kind of cover story—" Sturdley suddenly looked into John's eyes, every bit the stern uncle. "And where is she going to stay, may I ask?"

"We're at a hotel in La Jolla," John began, then stopped as he saw Sturdley's eyebrows rise. "In separate rooms. She thought the refund on the air fare should cover it."

"So that's all taken care of."

John's shoulders hunched again. "Except for getting her in here at the convention. I was hoping maybe you could help."

"Hey, Sturdley!"

Harry looked over to see a pot-bellied guy all in black—jeans, T-shirt, cowboy boots, even the baseball cap on his head. A greasy salt-and-pepper ponytail poked from the rear of the cap, flying back as the man ran toward them. "Lord protect us from the fanboys," Harry muttered, grabbing John's arm and heading toward the elevator.

"I thought you liked fans," John said in puzzlement.

"Some are harder to like than others," Harry replied. "That's Loony Lonnie Lancaster. He considers himself a superfan because he gets published in the occasional letter column. A legend in his own mind, and a major pain in the—"

The elevator didn't arrive, but Loony Lonnie did. "I'm talking to you, Sturdley," he said, his voice like a nasal buzz saw. "Why did you kill off Echo in *Mr.*

Pain? Don't you realize that she was the most original creation in comics today? Sheer poetry. Romance, a lover with psychic powers to help the crippled hero *feel* again, and what do you do? Bump her off! You're getting as bad as that Colby guy over at Dynasty."

"The Echo thing was Burke's call, not mine," Harry said.

"I dunno. It sounds like Harry's Heavy Hand to me," Loony Lonnie complained. "Now, how about these rumors that you're going to kill off the Glamazon?"

Harry's eyebrows rose. "Why should that upset you? I thought you hated the character."

"I've hated everything you've created in the last ten years," the fan told him bluntly. "But I hear you're sticking Burke onto that miniseries. Why? Don't you realize the whole comics world is waiting with bated breath for *Latter-Day Breed?* And instead you've got him wasting his time on this hack crap."

The elevator finally arrived, and Sturdley gratefully pulled John aboard. "Sorry I can't talk anymore, Lancaster. We have some business to take care of downstairs."

Loony Lonnie peered at John's name tag. "Oh, you're the guy doing *The Amazing Robert.* I wanna ask you—when are we gonna start seeing supervillains in that book? I mean, the adventures are so lame!"

"B-but they're based on real life—" John began.

"We'll discuss it later," Sturdley called as the elevator doors closed.

As the cab began moving, he looked at John with an eloquent face. "See what I mean, kid?"

John leaned against the wall, taking a deep breath. "Are all your fans like him?"

Harry smiled. "No, most of them are very nice."

John relaxed a little, until Harry went on. "Some, of course, are more pathological."

Sturdley smiled at his protégé's worried face. "I think you did a good thing, bringing Peg here. We'll probably need somebody to run interference for you."

Down by the check-in desk at the pro's entrance, Peg Faber stood waiting in increasing discomfort. More artists were arriving, and it began to feel like full moon at the Fantasy Factory's offices. Peg took it for granted that all artists were horny, but at least at the office most of the guys knew her now. She didn't know any of these guys, and they were staring at her the way jackals eye raw meat.

Three guys were waiting for a fourth to finish the check-in procedure, and Peg found herself shuddering under their gaze. It was as if their hot eyes shot out rays that were dissolving her clothing. And their conversation was hardly pleasant to listen to.

"Man, you should have stayed for the end of the opening party," a tall, slender guy with an eagle beak of a nose said. His name tag announced him as Rafe Lake, and Peg knew the name. He was the guy drawing the new *Ram-man* series for Dynasty comics. Now he was strutting like a peacock. "We went to this bar afterward, and there was this chick, a fangirl—"

The guy beside him, a dark-haired, good-looking type a little too aware of it, cut Lake off with a laugh. "Why do you think I cut out? I picked up one for myself early." Peg recognized the name on his tag, too—he was Hank Mannesman, artist on the hot new independent comic, *The Sproing*.

"Hey, I scored earlier than either of you," the third member of the group said. He was another independent comics artist, Steve Corliss, who drew *Starwitch*. "This cute little wench was like laying for me in the hotel lobby." He put his hands in his pockets, jutting his hips forward. "Nice."

Corliss glanced over at Peg. "That's nice, too," he added in a voice that carried a little farther than he realized. "I wouldn't mind—"

"Aaaaaah, she doesn't compare to what I had last night," Lake cut him off. "She was a tall blonde, on the lean side—"

"Hey, if you like skinny women," Corliss told him. "That was the only problem with the blonde I had last night. Nothing up *here*."

"You shoulda seen this blond bimbo from the party," Mannesman put in. "On the thin side, but *intense*." He leered. "She had this little mole, and when I touched it, it was like hitting her *on* button . . ."

His voice faltered as he peers' faces went pale. Mannesman silently reached over with his right hand to touch a spot on his right ribs. The three stared at each other for a long second.

"Oh," Lake groaned.

"My," Corliss chimed in.

"God!" Mannesman yelled.

Peg had to bite her lip to keep from laughing. Each of their hot babes had been the same person!

"Fangirls," Lake muttered.

The man at the check-in rose and turned around. Peg recognized the name on his card, too. Daniel Esteban was a West Coast artist who drew *The Masked Prickle* for the Fantasy Factory. His handsome, tanned face squinched as he stared for a second, then broke into a big smile. "Peg Faber! We met a couple of months ago when I was in New York." He turned to the others. "Have you met—?"

The other artists went even paler as they realized that the woman they'd been ogling was Harry Sturdley's assistant. They managed weak smiles and waves, scared to death that they'd never be able to sell anything to the Fantasy Factory.

With perfect timing, the elevator doors opened and Harry himself stepped out. The three stud-meisters were almost falling over themselves to make their escapes without seeming too rude. Esteban looked baffled as his friends all but carried him into the elevator.

"Welcome aboard, Red," Sturdley said, walking up to Peg. He glanced over his shoulder at the retreating artists. "They giving you any trouble?"

"Nah." Peg shook her head, grinning. "They were just embarrassing themselves."

Harry arranged for Peg's credentials, assigning her the job of shepherding John through the convention.

"How can I do that?" she asked. "I've never been to this madhouse before."

"Just protect him from the weirdos," Sturdley told her with a grin. "While he protects you from the artists."

"That might be a good exchange," Peg admitted.

Harry put up one hand. "We have to remember that a lot of serious business goes on at these conventions. Collectors buy fortunes worth of classic comics, awards are given, and the occasional deal gets made." He glanced over at John. "You're on one of the panel discussions, aren't you, kid?"

John nodded. "We're supposed to talk about the future of comics. The organizers thought that what we're doing with the heroes—reality reporting—was very interesting."

Sturdley turned back to Peg. "So you see, it's not all craziness."

The elevator finally arrived, and as they boarded, someone yelled, "Hold that, please!"

Two more passengers joined them. Harry recognized the harried-looking guy with the deep tan and the clipboard as a convention staffer. With him was a young, sandy-haired man whose name tag identified him as Scott Phelan.

"It's a pleasure to meet you, Mr. Sturdley," Phelan said, shaking hands. "I'm just starting out in publishing."

"Comics?" Harry asked politely.

"Graphic novels," Phelan explained. "My primary interest is anime."

Sturdley blinked. "Annie Mae who?"

"No—Japanimation." Phelan saw that he still wasn't coming across. "Japanese cartoons. There's a wide range of subject matter, from cutesie-poo kiddie stuff to more adult material, which is where I'm concentrating. Videocassettes, then books."

"Really," Sturdley said, interested.

Phelan nodded. "I've just bought the American rights for *NFN,* to issue a translated version. During the course of the convention, I'll be checking the dealers with police and Federal marshals to confiscate any bootleg copies of the Japanese videos. They're violating copyright law."

"Sounds very impressive." Sturdley glanced over at Peg. *See*? his look seemed to say. *This convention is serious business.*

"Excuse me, Mr. Phelan," Peg asked, but what does *NFN* stand for? Is it your company?"

"No, it's a very popular series of animated videos, *Naked Female Ninjas*. It's about two female assassins, one blonde, one a redhead, who always lose their clothes in the course of their missions . . ."

Phelan continued to describe the plot twists, while Peg looked at Sturdley with barely concealed laughter.

"Sounds *very* serious," she muttered.

CHAPTER 8

Joey Santangelo couldn't think of a situation where he'd felt more embarrassed. It was the second day of the San Diego Comics Con, and thousands of people were standing around him on the general admission line. That they were looking at him in admiration didn't help.

Joey was in costume, and he hated it.

They had arrived in San Diego the day before, on the flight right after the one John Cameron was supposed to take. Antony Carron had brought all his bodyguards. They'd managed to find a suite in a hotel miles away from the convention. Then had come the tedious job of trying to track down John Cameron. He wasn't in the hotel where the giants had said he'd be staying. But a check at the convention center confirmed that he was in attendance. He'd picked up his name tag.

Earlier, the sound of cracking knuckles had filled the suite like gunshots. Carron had been thrown off his plan and didn't like it. "We don't know where he is, or where he's going," the gang leader muttered angrily. "But we know where he's got to be. We'll just have to waste him on the convention floor."

The question was, how could five men with guns get

onto the convention floor? Carron had been watching the TV coverage of the convention when he saw two gaily dressed figures being interviewed. The first was a young guy who had a little too much gut for the outfit he was wearing.

"No, I don't think I'll ever come back again as Mr. Pain," he said, looking down at the abbreviated black-and-blue costume he was wearing. "People keep poking me and asking me if I feel it. I had one kid trying to stick me with a *pin*."

The other costumed conventioneer was a rather plain-faced girl whose bountiful body was squeezed into a rather brief Glamazon costume. "I love it!" she brayed, her cheeks pink with excitement. "A whole bunch of famous artists have asked me out." She giggled at the camera.

Antony Carron stared at the hotel television, his hands frozen in midcrunch. "Costumes," he'd said with hooded eyelids. "That's how we'll get in."

Joey was already on the phone, trying to score some handguns in town. Carron had been the weapons king of the East Coast, but his people hadn't been able to bring guns on the plane. He finished his business, then went to report. "I've lined up four Nines and an Uzi."

"I suppose we can bring the pistols in under our jackets, maybe a briefcase for the Uzi," Joey went on.

"Do you see people with jackets and briefcases in there?" Carron asked, pointing to the screen. "But in costumes we could wear masks so nobody saw our faces." He turned to his bodyguards. "Any of you remember comic-book guys with guns?"

"*Mick Ayer and the Agents of A.E.G.I.S.*—they were

secret agents and always carried guns," Harris, a tall, thin black guy, suggested.

"They didn't have comics where I came from," Nildo had said.

Sam, a big, brawny guy of indeterminate origin, frowned as he tried to cudgel his memory. "I usta read about Zenith, the Man of Molybdenum," he said. "There was a bunch of guys from other planets who drove around in spaceships trynta to waste him. They'd steer chunks of Molybdenite to hit the Earth and were always zapping him with ray guns and stuff."

Harris nodded his head. "Yeah, they wore cool black uniforms and had a weird name. The Kill Zenith Squad or Death to Zenith—"

"The Anti-Zenith Death Squad!" Sam said excitedly. "That was it."

"That's how we'll get into this convention," Carron said with a thin smile. "Except we'll be the John Cameron Death Squad."

Now Joey, Carron, Nildo, Harris, and Sam all stood in skintight black getups with holstered weapons, waiting to gain admission to the convention. Black cowls like ski masks covered their faces, except for Harris, who wore a green alien head.

Joey Santangelo had never felt so conspicuous in all his life, especially since the comics fans on line kept coming over to make comments.

"Nice costume, dude!" a young collector said, complimenting the costume. "Can I check out the blast-gun?"

"Sorry," Joey lied, "I got it glued into the holster."

He and the others had spent the past evening gluing garish bits and pieces from toy guys onto their real weapons, trying to disguise them. Joey thought it made his automatic look like a real pimp-gun, but when the boss ordered it, he figured he'd better go along.

Streams of sweat were running down under Joey's costume by the time they were in range of the ticket windows. But when he saw the security checkpoint beyond, the stream became a flood.

"What do we do if they search us?" he whispered to Carron.

"We hope that doesn't happen," Carron whispered back.

Just as they reached the security people, there was a commotion farther back in the line.

"Coming through!" a crisp female voice announced.

Joey turned to see the blonde with the nice butt who used to be on *First News* come marching up with a camera crew—Leslie Ann Whatsername.

Security people and ticket takers clustered around. "These people are press," a heavyset guy with a blond ponytail and a black suit told the convention officials. He had some kind of name tag on his jacket lapel—Marty Burke.

The security guy frowned. "We don't have I.N.C. on our comp list."

Leslie Ann came over to confront him. "Look, buster," she said, pointing to the I.N.C. logo on the side of the camera. "We're International News Combine. *Network* news. If you think the convention people don't want national coverage—"

"I didn't say that," the security guy said with a cheerful smile. Joey turned in his ticket and stepped behind the guard. Carron followed. In moments the whole crew was onto the convention floor while the newswoman still argued.

"Come on," Carron muttered through his stifling

cowl. "I don't want those TV people coming through and shooting pictures of us."

He gave a hollow chuckle. "After all, we've got shooting of our own to do."

Letting his henchmen cut a way through the crowd for him, Carron began leafing through the convention program. "Cameron is supposed to be making a speech or something. Yes. Here he is. There's a panel on 'The Future of Comics' this afternoon."

The black cloth of his mask hid the shark's smile. "We'll be there."

"Where are those guys in the black costumes?" Leslie Ann Nasotrudere said, staring into the crowd thronging the aisles of the convention. "They'd have made a nice establishing shot."

Leslie Ann had covered dozens of conventions in her day, from rowdy law-enforcement bashes to consumer-electronics shows featuring porn stars. But she'd never seen a convention quite like this one.

It was an amazing scene. The football-field-size convention hall was filled with two thousand booths containing everything from comics to costumes, collectible kitsch and valuable original artwork from famous comics.

The convention attendees were a polyglot assortment, visitors from fifty countries mingling with comics professionals and Hollywood moguls looking for their next high-concept property. Leslie Ann saw harried single parents either with children in tow or chasing after wayward charges. Some of the daddies were distracted by beautiful girls in superheroine-skimpy bikinis, distributing handbills directing convention at-

tendees to various booths or announcing special events and autograph sessions.

The convention-goers seemed equally divided among males and females, kids and adults, Americans and foreigners, humans and aliens—in costumes, Leslie Ann fervently hoped.

Huge displays topped or framed the exhibits of the larger comics publishers. The newswoman's eye was caught by the twenty-foot-high Zenith balloon soaring over the Dynasty Comics tables, and the huge neon-tube sculpture of the Sproing that cast a garish light over the artists at the Umbrage Comics booth.

And throughout the gigantic floor area, thousands upon thousands of comics fans and collectors roamed the aisles, looking for their next purchase, the ultimate bargain, or that rare missing issue to fill in their run of *The Petulant Lump* from 1966.

She turned to Marty Burke and gave him a bright smile. "This is perfect."

"It is the largest," he said proudly.

But Leslie Ann was still speaking. "It's like a real freak show," she gloated. "If Sturdley brings one of the giants into this, I'll be able to show him up as the most crass sonofabitch in all history."

"From what I understand, Thomas will perform in the plaza down by the docks," Burke said.

"It won't matter. We can intercut footage of this carnival with whatever he does. Is Sturdley really going to have him do a strongman act?" Leslie Ann couldn't believe her enemy would play into her hands this way.

"Unless there's been a last-minute change of plans, he'll be doing weight lifting this afternoon, after the panel discussion."

Leslie Ann's teeth seemed sharper than usual as she smiled. "I can hardly wait."

But she was all business as she turned to her crew. "We need somebody in costume to kick this off," she said. "And, of course, we'll use you, Marty."

"Owwww, you guys! Quit it!" an annoyed voice rang over the crowd noise as a pudgy guy in a too-small black-and-blue costume flew out of one of the aisles, rubbing his butt cheeks. Several giggling teenagers trailed after him.

"I thought you weren't supposed to feel that pinch!" one of them called after the masked man.

"Excuse me," Leslie Ann said to the costumed figure, unlimbering her microphone. "Could you come over here and talk to us for a moment?"

"There's supposed to be a costume parade in a little while, and I was already on TV," the young man began. Then he spotted Burke's name tag.

"*Marty Burke!*" he cried in a voice usually reserved for presidents and religious figures. The guy in the Mr. Pain costume rushed over and began pumping Burke's hand. "I love you! You're a genius! I hated *Mr. Pain* when Thibault was doing it. He was just running the book into the ground. But since you took over—wow! Mr. Pain is my favorite character."

The pudgy guy leaned forward. "But how are you going to bring Echo back? She was great. There's a guy walking around saying she's the best creation in *years.*"

Burke smiled and tried to extricate his fingers, wondering if the crew was getting the scene on tape. Is this what Leslie Ann wanted? This guy sounded pretty sensible. A crowd was gathering behind them as more and more people muttered Burke's name.

"Yeah, look, it's Marty Burke!" somebody said.

"Hey, Burke, when is *Latter-Day Breed* coming out?" another called.

Raucous noises burst out as the crowd lost all restraint. Leslie Ann's attempted interview with the costumed young man was drowned out.

"Why'd you kill off Echo?"

"Can I have your autograph?"

The guy in the Mr. Pain costume abruptly came out of his hero-worship. "Me first," he said. "Could you sign . . ."

He felt frantically around the pocketless, tiny costume for something autographable. "Damn, what a time to be without my books," he said.

Finally, the guy would up tearing off a glove. "Could you sign my hand?" he begged.

The conference room was large and crowded, but respectfully silent as the moderator of the panel looked down the table on the dais. He was a heavyset, horse-faced man with a fringe of gray hair. His nametag introduced him as Rip Jacoby, and he'd gotten a standing ovation when he'd launched the panel thirty minutes earlier.

"Well," Jacoby said, "this panel has been a real eye-opener for me. The future of comics looks pretty bright, whether it's Walt Cochran's idea for comics on CD-ROM—"

"Gigabytes of art! Theme music! Multimedia!" a bespectacled young man in the middle of the panel burst out enthusiastically.

The veteran illustrator and moderator gave Cochran what seemed to be an indulgent smile, but his voice relentlessly overrode the interruption. "To our young friend, John Cameron, doing comics based on real life."

John's boyish face colored a little as he acknowledged the recognition with a nod.

In the audience, Peg turned to Harry Sturdley in puzzlement. "What's the big news in comics with theme music? Haven't cartoons done that for years?"

"Save that for the question-and-answer session," Sturdley whispered back with an evil smile. "I'd like to see what Cochran has to say to that."

He shrugged. To date, digital comics had not been a great success. They required a big up-front investment in hardware and software, making for a cover price that would buy a nice dinner in many cities. Most comics fans were much happier plunking down a couple of bucks for their monthly superhero fix.

Sturdley smiled as he looked up at the panel. John had handled himself well in the discussion, speaking enough but not too much about the hero comics. Harry would have to thank Rip Jacoby after this was over. He'd asked his co-worker of years ago to look after John on the panel. Jacoby had done an outstanding job.

"We've got about twenty minutes left," Jacoby said, looking out over the seated audience. "I think the time has come for questions. Just raise your hands—ah, the gentleman in the back."

A figure dressed all in black rose in the rear. Judging from the empty seats on either side of him, Loony Lonnie apparently hadn't changed from yesterday's outfit.

The fan smiled and tipped back his black baseball cap. "I've got a question for John Cameron."

Sturdley's heart sank. But up on the dais, John

straightened up, then leaned toward the microphone. "I'll do my best to answer it."

"You've gone on quite a bit about how this Robert character has surprised you with his powers," Loony Lonnie said. "My question is this: If Robert and Jumboy had a fight, who would win?"

John sat for a moment with his mouth hanging open. Then he jerked himself together and leaned toward the mike. "As I said earlier in the panel, our license with the heroes extends only to covering their real-life exploits. And fighting crime in New York gives us plenty of material—some of it pretty unbelievable, although it's all true. But there won't be any supervillains in *The Amazing Robert, The Fabulous Barbara, The Titanic Thomas,* or *The Rampaging Ruth*—not unless someone out there decides to put on a costume and give it a try."

He took a deep breath, carefully trying to be courteous. "Because of the reality clause, we can't bring in characters from the Fantasy Factory galaxy like Jumboy, for the same reason we can't have him come here and visit today. He's a great character, but—well, he's not real."

"I understand all that," Lonnie said impatiently. "But if it *could* happen, who'd turn out to be stronger?"

John shook his head, momentarily at a loss for words, confronting the loops of Lancaster's fan logic. Then he grinned. "I guess that would depend on who was drawing the action," he finally said. "If Zeb Grantfield had the pen, I wouldn't be surprised if Jumboy won. But if it was up to me, Robert would whup Jumboy's butt."

"But how could that be?" Lonnie objected. "Jumboy

is the biggest badass in the Fantasy Factory galaxy. He'd fight dirty—"

"Excuse me." Rip Jacoby drowned out the rest of the fan's tirade with his amplified voice. "We'll have to move on to some other questions—time is getting short. How about this gentleman up in the right front. You had your hand up."

The little guy with a laptop computer under his arm asked Walk Cochran a highly technical question about picture compression ratios in computers.

Peg turned to her boss. "Well, I think he came through that pretty well," she said. "He did his best to make sense of a weird question, and pretty well got off the hook." She glanced dubiously back to where Loony Lonnie stood, still waving his hand.

Good luck on having the moderator call *you* again, she thought.

On the dais, John sank back in his seat, looking visibly relieved to be out of the spotlight.

When the panel ended, many of the fans headed for the front of the room rather than the exit. Some hoped to have a few words one-on-one with their favorite artist. Others were looking to get autographs without having to wait on one of the official—and usually endless—autograph lines.

John gathered up his things and began to rise, when a pretty young woman walked over and said, "Mr. Cameron? Can I talk to you for a minute, please? My name is Tawny. I'm thrilled to meet you." She seized John's hand and squeezed it. Tawny was perfectly named, her abundant hair flowing like a silken lion's mane. She was in that late-twenties-early-thirties area, glowing with the confidence and charm of a mature woman, but glorying in a body that was still firm and smooth—lusciously displayed by the tight T-shirt and snug-fitting cutoffs she wore.

Moving as if in a dream, John casually linked arms with Tawny and drifted to a corner of the room.

"I'm a big fan of yours, Mr. Cameron. I know that sounds strange since you've only had a couple of books published, but—"

"Oh . . . uh, call me John, please. You're really nice . . ." John began to stammer. "I mean . . . it's, uh . . . that's really nice of you."

"The premiere issue of *Robert* really blew me away!" Tawny said, her big blue eyes staring directly into his. "You have such a great style. I can see a little Marty Burke in your figure work, and some Grantfield in your layouts. But what about your other influences? I suspect you've studied Frazetta, and it looks like you're also a fan of John Buscema's work from the seventies."

John grinned. "You got me," he admitted.

From across the room, Peg Faber made a beeline through the crowd. God, she thought, I can't leave John alone for a minute! It's not enough fending off the crazies, now I have to protect him from fan-girls, too. I hope she's not the one the other artists were talking about! She's probably just given him her room number—written on her panties, no doubt. And she's old enough to be his mother!

By the time Peg arrived at the scene of the crime, she found John now talking to both the blond woman and a young boy, about eight years old. When John saw Peg, he smiled and waved her over. "Peg! Over here! Peg Faber, this is Tawny . . . and her son Harold."

"Glad to meet you, Ms. Faber. Say hello, Harold."

The boy glowed with the same confidence as his mother. But when he extended his hand and spoke, Peg was surprised by the boy's volume and pronunciation—he was either totally deaf or seriously hearing-impaired.

"Tawny's a nurse at the Children's Hospital here, Peg. And Harold's a big fan of the hero books."

"I am too!" the young woman assured him. She bent down to face Harold, and spoke not too slowly but quite distinctly, "I'm afraid we'll have to leave Mr. Cameron now, honey. He's a busy man. Maybe we can see him again before the convention is over. We'd better scoot if we want good seats for those artists doing the makeover on the Lump!"

"Cool!" Harold cried in his odd, atonal voice. "But don't forget you're supposed to give him—"

"Oh, right!" Tawny dug into a satchel-sized handbag. "The kids at the hospital made me promise to give this to you." She took out a large, folded piece of paper and gave it to John. "Thanks, John—Ms. Faber. I hope to see you both later." With a final wave, Tawny set off after her son, leaving John with the oversized, slightly crumpled piece of construction paper.

Peg gave John a questioning look. "Well," she said, "open it up."

Unfolded, the construction paper was filled with crayon drawings of Robert copied from John's comics. At the top, in a child's scrawl, as the legend: *To Robert and John. We love you both.* At the bottom of the paper were the signatures of a dozen kids.

"Tawny!" he took off after the woman. She glanced back. "Your children's ward—is there some clean, blank wall space there?"

Tawny blinked. "What for?"

John gave her a shy smile. "Like for a mural of superheroes?"

Face shining, Tawny nodded and disappeared into the crowd.

"She's quite a woman," John finally said to Peg. "Between her work at the hospital, and Harold's special schooling . . . and she's alone, too. Her husband abandoned them when he found out that Harold had a birth defect."

Peg found her vision suddenly clouded by moisture. "It's nice to know that people like Tawny read comics too. That our work is doing some good out in the world." She flung an arm around John. "And you ain't so bad yourself." Together, they headed in the direction of the door. "Now let's catch up to Harry before he decides we're deserted him and signed on with Dynasty Comics."

The area outside the conference rooms was empty right now, but Antony Carron knew that in moments it would be full of people. The panel discussion would be breaking up, and this was the hallway that led back to the convention floor. He'd placed his people carefully. They wanted to get a crossfire on John Cameron, but he didn't want his gunmen worrying about being hit by their fellow assassins.

Now it was all done, except for the waiting. Carron adjusted his gaudily decorated Uzi on its shoulder strap and aimed down the hall. Squeeze the trigger, spray the hallway, then run for the nearest emergency exit. Joey Santangelo was already downstairs, with the getaway car purring.

Piece of cake, Carron thought to himself.

Sam glanced at the anachronistic wristwatch he wore over his costume's glove. "Where are they?" he muttered tensely.

"Just get ready," was Carron's terse reply.

From up the hallway, they suddenly heard the babble of voices approaching. The doors to the conference room must have opened. Carron braced himself.

The crowd headed for the convention floor, a tall, gawky acne-scarred guy in the lead, talking to a pot-bellied character dressed in all black. Carron scanned the faces in the assemblage, trying to match the one from the surveillance photos he'd taken of John Cameron. There he was, in the middle of the crowd, a cute little redhead on his arm. Carron raised his Uzi. His first shot would be the signal for the others.

He was distracted by loud voices from behind him. "I tell ya, Grantfield," the guy in black was saying, "your guy could kick the shit out of this Robert wimp."

Young, gawky Zeb Grantfield blushed bright red behind his acne. "Lonnie, you're a loyal fan," he said, reaching into a satchel slung over his shoulder. "And I have a reward for loyal fans. Here's some copies of *Jumboy* Number One, autographed!"

He gave one to the black-clad guy, then began tossing the others at random into the crowd. The reaction was a low roar.

"*Jumboy* Number One! That's worth a hundred bucks with an autograph!"

"Hey! Grantfield! Over here! I always loved Jumboy!" someone else yelled.

"I'll take one," another fan screamed.

"Me! Me!"

The crowd became a mob, dashing forward to grab the collectors' items.

Carron managed to get the safety back on his gun as he and his carefully positioned assassins were swept away in a mad rush of fans.

CHAPTER 9

Bloody murder shone in Carron's eyes as he fought the movement of the crowd around him. Of all the lousy luck. That idiot tossing around comics was going to cause a riot, if he wasn't careful.

The gray-haired guy who'd been talking with Cameron pushed through the mob, ordering them back. Then he started chewing out Grantfield.

"What do you think you're doing? Start a rush like that, and the next thing you know, somebody gets knocked over and stepped on."

"I just wanted to show that I appreciated—" Grantfield began.

"You just wanted to show off for Loony Lonnie and the other fans," Harry Sturdley cut him off. "Well, grow up. Show's over, folks! No more freebies. Spread out."

I've got one last chance, Carron thought. Cameron can't have gotten away in this mob scene. If I can locate him, I can still blow him away.

Fans reluctantly moved away, and the crowd parted. There, where people were still congregated the thickest, was John Cameron and the redhead. Shame to shoot her too, but you don't make money without breaking eggs, Carron told himself. And the money he'd make from this hit would handsomely tide him over until the gun business picked up again.

Carron raised the Uzi. Then, over his shoulder, he heard a voice yelling, "There! There's one of them!"

Dropping the gun to his side, Carron whipped around. A sandy-haired guy with a mustache was heading straight for him, flanked by two tough-looking types in khaki police uniforms and a couple of guys in suits that yelled *cop*!

Word got out somehow, a paranoid voice whispered in the back of Carron's brain. The law caught Joey in a no-parking zone, and he spilled everything. As Antony Carron decided whether to make a run for it or play Dodge City and shoot it out, the shouting man and his uniformed minions suddenly veered left.

A scared-looking guy in one of the dealer's booths dithered as the angry guy produced legal papers. "We're confiscating every copy of *NFN* we find here," the sandy-haired man said in a loud voice. "I'm the only one in this country with the rights to those videos. If you want to sell them, you've got to buy them from my company. Got it?"

As he spoke, the two law-and-order types pawed through the collection of the dealer's videotapes, taking some and stashing them in a plastic garbage bag.

Chuckling, Carron shook his head. He had no idea what the hell was going on, but he knew one thing all too well. He and his men couldn't waste John Cameron with two cops standing right beside them. They'd have to trail him and wait for another opportunity.

Carron turned back to the crowd, which had almost completely dispersed. A little knot still stood around Zeb Grantfield. The gray-haired man was scanning the crowd as well, looking puzzled.

Antony Carron thought he knew why.

John Cameron and his redheaded friend had disappeared.

Peg Faber took another mouthful of fruit salad and savored the fresh sweetness. They were out in the garden of their hotel, enjoying the view from the top of a promontory jutting into the Pacific Ocean. Peg wore shorts and a sleeveless T-shirt, and she shivered a little in the ocean breeze.

John Cameron slipped off his jacket. "Here," he said, "I'm better insulated."

"You took a big risk," she told him as she slipped the jacket over her shoulders. "Somebody could have seen us Rifting out of the middle of that crowd."

"Everybody's eyes were on Zeb Grantfield and his free offer," John said. He hunched his shoulders down. "I just didn't want to be caught in the middle of a mob."

"I'm surprised you didn't go back and get Harry out, too."

John looked a little guilty. "If I'd done that, he'd have been here with us—and I kind of wanted a quiet lunch for two."

Peg pulled the jacket a bit more tightly around herself. "You're full of surprises, John Cameron."

His lips quirked in a rueful smile. "Yeah, I'm a regular man of mystery."

Peg's eyes regarded him steadily. "The last time we had this conversation, the game was called on account of rampaging giants."

"I've been thinking about that a lot," John said. "And I've decided you should know the truth." He ran a hand through his thick brown hair, his eyes seemingly focused on the burger that stood untouched on the plate in front of him.

"If you think I'm a mystery to you, it's because I'm pretty much a mystery to *myself*."

Peg put down her fork. "What?"

"My first memory is standing naked in the middle of a forest road," John sent on. "That was about two years ago. I didn't know who I was, even *what* I was. After wandering through the woods for a while, I came on the outskirts of the town of Cameron Corners. I spied on people, stole clothes from wash lines, and eventually learned English."

"You spoke another language?" Peg said, dumbstruck.

"I didn't speak any language at all." John put his hands together, lacing his fingertips. "But I learned fast—incredibly quickly, I know now. The same way I learned to write." He shrugged. "Maybe I was . . . remembering."

"And your name?"

"I made it up. Cameron from Cameron Corners, and John—well, that's a common name."

"But you don't know who you are," Peg said quietly.

John shrugged again, trying to make light of it. "I don't know who I *was*." Then his expression darkened. "I don't so much mind the nonsense that goes with not officially existing—not having credit cards or a bank account."

Peg nodded. Until she'd gotten to know him, John had lived entirely in the cash economy. He'd had other people cash his paychecks, and the social security number that the Fantasy Factory had registered his taxes under belonged to a dead man. Peg had found this out shortly after the first giants had appeared in

New York. Robert and Maurice had made a deal with Harry Sturdley, giving him absolute licensing control if he could get John Cameron to open the Rift and bring more of their people to this world.

The only problem was that John had disappeared from the face of the Earth—literally. Peg, Elvio Vital, and Marty Burke been the search party that tried to track him down. All they'd discovered was that the past John Cameron had presented to everyone at the Fantasy Factory was a lie.

"I'm making too much money now," John went on. "I'll have to pay taxes, which means I've got to come back in from the cold." The look he gave Peg wasn't very boyish—it was scared. "I've got to try and find out who I was."

"Is that so bad?" she asked.

"What if I don't like that person?" John said. "What if I'm a crook, or a creep . . . or" —he stumbled over the word. "Or m-married?"

They sat very still over barely touched plates, stricken into silence. Then Peg grabbed his hand. "Then maybe you . . . we . . . ought to know."

She thought for a second. "You remember that man who just waltzed into Harry's office a few weeks ago? Well, it turns out he's a private detective. I stumbled across some invoices from Farley Investigations, something about surveillance. Maybe we can talk to him, have him backtrack on any people who may have disappeared near Cameron Corners—"

"That's a good idea," John said, squeezing her fingers. "You're very good to me."

"But it would be better if you lovebirds finished your meals and got going." a familiar voice griped above them.

They pulled their hands away to find Harry Sturdley glaring down at them.

"I figured this is where you'd turn up after you disappeared at the convention." He waved a finger at John. "You owe me cabfare out here—and a free ride back."

Harry glanced at his watch. "Take a few more bites, settle the check, and let's get moving. Our big promotion is due to start in fifteen minutes." He raised a hand. "And don't try to beg off. You're a famous artist now, and you're expected to do sketches and autographs."

Peg stood up to model her outfit. "I'll come along to help—and catch some rays. This is set up outdoors, right?"

"Yeah. If Thomas screws up while juggling a Volvo, I'd rather have it fall on pavement than go through a floor."

Peg's mouth opened wide. "He's really going to be juggling a Volvo?"

Harry smiled. "I don't want to give away the climax of the act, but it does involve him picking up a car—a large, solid one."

Bright southern California sunshine was beating down on the open space where the Fantasy Factory was going to stage its promotional show. The dockside plaza, a five-minute walk from the convention, was dominated by a parked Volvo, where Thomas would do his stuff. Blocking off that area was a line of tables with chairs behind them, where Fantasy Factory luminaries would dispense sketches and autographs.

Leslie Ann Nasotrudere looked over the locale like a general scouting a battlefield. "This is where we'll set up the camera," she said decisively. "There's a microphone over there—maybe we can catch Sturdley being fatuous, a further part of his abuse of the giants."

"I hear they shipped Thomas cross-country in a moving van," Marty Burke offered helpfully. He felt torn, wanting very much to be in the picture when they filmed, but not sure that was a good place to be if this turned into a scathing exposé.

He finally decided on taking a seat barely in frame, just in case. "I suppose they'll want the middle seats for their big new stars, anyway," he said bitterly. "Nagel, Grantfield, and, of course, *John Cameron.*"

Neither he nor Leslie Ann paid much attention to the costumed figure with the ray gun slung from its shoulder. But the eyes in the slit of the face-covering cowl were narrowed in thought.

Gazing over the crowd from behind his sunglasses, Harry Sturdley was pleased to see that the Fantasy Factory's promotion was going even better than he'd hoped. A large crowd had gathered to watch Thomas do his warm-up exercises, and hundreds of people were already lined up at the artists' tables.

I'm glad now we didn't pipe in the circus music, Harry decided. It would have been too tacky.

He glanced along the line of artists interacting with the fans. All was going well. Elvio Vital was doodling off quick caricatures of the Electrocutioner every couple of seconds, it seemed. John Cameron took a little longer with his pictures of Robert, but he personalized each one. At the bottom of the page, in perfect scale with the twenty-foot-tall giant, was an amazing likeness of the fan who was going to get the sketch. Peg was farther down the line, distributing some promotional fliers.

Coming to a stop behind John, Harry noticed that the kids' sketchbook was open on the table. There were more studies of that enigmatic cityscape with the cloud-topped towers and the flying figures. One was a detailed sketch, the head and shoulders of someone wrapped in futuristic-looking armor. This had to be another world that John had visited through the Rift—a world with human-size heroes!

Wouldn't it be a coup to add *that* to the Fantasy Factory galaxy? Harry thought.

"Kid," he said to the busily drawing young artist, "have you visited any other places through the, ah—you know?"

John looked back at Sturdley after a quick glance at the fan raptly paging through a promotional copy of next month's *Robert.*

"Some places are easier to get to than others," Cameron said. "There are currents in the"—he made an empty-handed gesture—"the whatever that's in there. If you just . . . hang out . . . you'll feel yourself being pulled in a certain direction. Sometimes it's to a place nearby. But other times, you can be pulled . . . well, let's just say far away."

Sturdley wanted to know more, but hesitated to insist on it. For some reason, he'd angered John the last time he'd pressed on the subject of this strange world in his sketches.

John handed a finished sketch to the next grateful fan, and Harry leaned forward. "But you *have* been to other places," he began.

"Hey there, guys," the buzz-saw voice of Loony Lonnie Lancaster greeted them as he stepped up, next in line. He'd changed out of his all black outfit and now wore a Jumboy costume, apparently getting ready for the big costume parade. To give an idea of his scale, Lonnie also carried a prop—a cardboard carton taller than he was, painted to look like a high-rise building.

Lonnie shook hands with John. "You did great on the panel—I loved your answer to my question. But it still didn't tell me where the heroes rank in the Fantasy Factory galaxy."

Doesn't this guy understand English? Sturdley wondered. "Under our contract—" he began.

"Oh, I understand the *policy*," Lonnie said. "But you've got to realize every fan will be wondering how these guys stack up against the fictional characters." He turned to John. "Could you give me a sketch of Robert and Jumboy arm-wrestling?"

"We just said—" Sturdley began again.

But John laughed. "Oh, come on, Mr. Sturdley—it's not for the book. Besides, I can understand Mr. Lancaster's feelings."

"That worries me," Harry muttered.

John was already sketching, a grin on his face. "Just remember, if I'm drawing it, you can bet Robert will be winning."

His marker flew over the paper, and Robert and Jumboy appeared, muscles bulging, looking as if they were locked in titanic conflict. Off in the corner, John added a miniature figure in black, waving a Jumboy banner—a perfect, tiny caricature of Loony Lonnie.

The fan burst out in appreciative laughter. "Sturdley, you should try this kid out on some of your other books," he said.

At that moment, Sturdley became aware of a disturbance farther back in the rank of fans.

"Hey," somebody yelled, "stop tryin' to push ahead."

Harry glanced up to see five figures in black costumes stepping out of the line.

"What are you guys doing here?" he asked with mock anger. "The Anti-Zenith Death Squad is a Dynasty Comics creation."

The Death Squad members drew their weapons.

"A joke's a joke," Sturdley said a bit more sharply. "Either get back in the line or get lost."

Loony Lonnie had turned to watch the altercation. Now he gasped. "Jeezus!" he yelled. "Those are real guns!"

The heavyset fan's response would have been worthy of the character whose costume he wore. Lonnie grabbed his cardboard-box "building" and flung it in the faces of the oncoming gunmen. Then he leapt forward.

Gunfire ripped through the air, but for a critical instant, the armed men were blinded by the flying box. Lonnie Lancaster tried an awkward tackle on one of the gunmen, who lashed out with the butt of his pistol. The fan lay on the ground, blood seeping from a gash on his temple.

John Cameron was already on his feet, grabbing Harry's arm as he overturned the table for some sort of cover. "Ohmigod!" Sturdley breathed as John dragged him behind the hopelessly frail shelter. Everything seemed to be moving in slow motion. The lines of fans dissolved in screaming panic, some people even blundering into the line of fire. The guys with the guns now raised their aim a little, shooting over the fans' heads in a grotesque crowd-control maneuver, trying to force everyone to duck down and give them a clear field of fire again.

Huddled behind the table, Harry flung a pleading shout to the performance space behind him. "Thomas! Thomas, do something—help us!" But the giant didn't seem to hear. He could read minds! Why hadn't he seen this coming? Why wasn't he moving to stop it?

Thomas stood in a pose of readiness, but he didn't move. He seemed to be waiting for something. The giant glanced down at John, and for a split second, his eyes met Harry's. With sick realization, Sturdley realized what the giant was waiting for.

My god, he thought, we've been set up.

Harry's voice rose in a scream, trying to pierce the cacophony of hysteria and gunfire. "We've got to Rift out of here!"

John paid no attention. He stared farther to their left, where Peg Faber still stood, frozen. Then John burst into action, pulling Harry with him across the line of fire to reach Peg.

Her face was pale with horror, but she came out of her daze, dropping to her knees to crawl toward them as one of the other artists kicked over another table for protection. There was still an open space between them. Peg dodged, Harry stumbled, and John lunged toward her.

As he was whipped around, Sturdley saw one of the gunmen shifting a heavier weapon off a shoulder sling. Behind that, held in absolute clarity, he saw Leslie Ann Nasotrudere yanking at her cameraman to cover them with his lens.

John caught Peg's hand, and three of them tumbled

behind the upended table. Then the Uzi erupted with a snarl of automatic fire.

Harry saw a patch of bright red blossom suddenly on John's shoulder.

At the same instant, he caught movement behind them—a dozen fans had made their way over to the area where Thomas still stood, and were pleading with him to do something. A few hid behind his legs, and one girl kept screaming, "Be a hero! Be a hero!" This seemed to galvanize Thomas into action. He snatched up the car he was supposed to use in his stunts and hurled it through the air. But instead of smashing the gunmen, it landed in the space between them and the upended tables. The Volvo crashed on its side, bullet holes stitching across its rear trunk.

Then the gas tank exploded.

Heat roared over Sturdley as if he were being flash-cooked. He remembered the nightmare flames that had licked across his body. Poking his head over their flimsy barricade, he took in a scene of pure horror. The center of the plaza was now clear of people except for the gunmen, who were running their way. The car was furiously ablaze, throwing off a choking cloud of burning plastics and tires. Sirens screamed from the far end of the open space as San Diego Police cruisers arrived.

Behind him, down on the docks, Sturdley heard the deep-throated roar of a powerboat's throttle being opened.

That must be how they expect to get out of here, he thought.

He ducked back down. John's eyes were open, but glassy. The bloodstain on his shirt spread with frightening speed. "Kid, they're coming for us," Harry croaked.

John raised wavering hands to grab hold of Harry and Peg.

Sturdley heard running footsteps and looked up just in time to see the gunmen vaulting tables as they fled the police. One of the black-clad figures spotted them and stopped, raising his pistol. A gust of wind blew coils of smoke between them.

John took a deep breath.

Then they were tumbling into the infinite emptiness of the Rift.

CHAPTER 10

Marty Burke and Leslie Ann Nasotrudere sat in their hotel room, staring at the television. For the fifth time, they replayed the tape that Leslie Ann's cameraman had shot.

The scene opened as Burke remembered it, the giant Thomas standing in the background ready to go into his act, the tables with Fantasy Factory luminaries giving their autographs. Burke actually walked into camera range, having left Leslie Ann and going to take a seat.

Then the guys in black costumes—the very ones Leslie Ann had wanted to interview earlier—drew their weapons and started shooting. The picture began to jink and waver as the cameraman was buffeted by terrified people trying to push past to safety. But incredibly, he managed to keep the focus where the action was.

Again, Burke saw that fan, Lonny Lancaster, launch his doomed counterattack before he was pistol-whipped. Then John Cameron knocked over the table and grabbed Sturdley. The kid had guts, he had to admit. Marty Burke wouldn't have wasted time trying to get Peg Faber under cover, much less Harry Sturdley.

But Cameron paid for his heroic impulse. Even as he

grabbed the girl's wrist, his body jerked, his face tightening as a bright red stain quickly spread down his right shoulder. They fell behind the table, then the Volvo flew into the frame, hurled by Thomas.

Both Burke and Leslie Ann winced at the explosion, and the picture spun, going out of focus as the cameraman was rammed by some out-of-control bystander fleeing the scene.

Leslie Ann stabbed a finger on the remote control and fast-forwarded.

"Okay," she said, "this is after Ernie got back up and was shooting again."

The plaza was just about empty. Thomas had stepped over the line of tables, and the gunmen had disappeared behind the wall of smoke rising from the ruined car. Several still forms lay sprawled on the expanse of concrete. Others moved cautiously—people who had hit the dirt. Police and paramedics came rushing onto the scene to treat the wounded. A paramedic shoved back the overturned table.

No one was behind it.

"That's where they fell when the camera was knocked away," Leslie Ann said definitely.

"Maybe they snuck out from behind it somehow," Burke suggested.

"Snuck where? That's the escape route the gunmen took." Leslie Ann shook her head. "They were there, now nobody can find them."

She turned to Marty.

"So where the hell did they go?"

Happy Harry Sturdley usually found the transition to the Rift traumatic enough. But this time, they seemed to *lurch* into the endless void. And they weren't just falling—they were tumbling. The sensation of erratic, uncontrolled movement made Sturdley's stomach threaten to rebel. Nothingness tugged at them as they spiraled inward—

And then, abruptly, they were sprawling on the marble floor of John Cameron's Grand Central Station of the Mind. Harry and Peg had both been there before. It had served as the halfway point between Earth and Robert's homeworld.

For his own esoteric reasons, Cameron claimed it helped him visualize the trip to different destinations. The difference between John's creation and the real Grand Central Station was that the replica was clean and new. To Sturdley's knowledge only fifty-three people had trodden the gleaming floors of its main gallery, as opposed to the millions of footsteps that had traversed the original.

Peg knelt beside John's still form, her face pale, her eyes enormous. But her voice was calm and steely. "We've got to get John over to a wall. Help me sit him up. We've got to keep the wound above the level of his heart." Peg's fingers were deft and gentle as she tore open his shirt's shoulder seam at the site of the wound.

"The blood's spurting," she said in a tight voice. "We've got an artery involved." Peg reached into her bag and took out a small plastic-wrapped package. From the logo, Sturdley recognized it as a sanitary napkin. She tore the package open, then flattened out the wrapping and spread it over John's wound, using the napkin itself as a pressı re pad.

"The bullet's still in there, and I don't think anything is broken. But there's no way I can stop this blood loss—only slow it down."

Harry licked suddenly dry lips. "Do you . . ." he let the words die out.

Peg glanced up at him. "Do I know what I'm doing? Well, I won a badge in lifesaving and first aid in the Girl Scouts." Her eyes went back to John. "Of course, back home we didn't get a whole lot of training in gunshot wounds. Our real problem is shock."

She loosened John's shirt and belt. His face was ashen gray, and his gaze was unfocused. Slowly, his eyes cleared and John inched his head around to look at Peg. "Chilly in here," he muttered feebly. His face was covered in cold sweat.

"Get out of that jacket," Peg told Harry. "We've got to keep him warm."

Wordlessly, Harry shucked off a sports jacket worth several hundred dollars and handed it over to Peg, who draped it over the wounded young man's body.

"This ought to help. Just lie still—you'll be fine," she told John, keeping her voice cheerful. But the face Peg turned to Sturdley was etched with concern.

"We've got him stabilized," she whispered. "What he really needs, though, is a doctor, and fast. If he gives in to the shock, he'll lose consciousness—maybe even go into a coma."

Harry looked in horror at the blood soaking through John's shirt. The kid's eyes were again unfocused, sort of staring through Peg.

An awful thought stuck Sturdley: If John were unconscious, he couldn't manipulate the Rift—and how would they got out of here? In fact, would *here* still be around? Did John's Grand Central of the Mind exist when his mind was unconscious?

The answer came a moment later, when the vaulted

ceiling high above them abruptly winked out of existence.

"Peg!" Harry said in a strangled voice. "If he's nodding off, wake him up again! This place is dissolving!"

The upper part of the walls shimmered, giving way to the dark nothingness of the Rift. Harry was reminded of a spun-sugar house he'd been given as a present once. With a glass of water, he'd melted away the walls, watching them slowly liquify and gather into a puddle of glistening sugar water.

As Harry cast panicky glances around, he saw that the wall above them was still solid, but the far end of the concourse had disappeared. Nothingness lapped toward them like a relentless tide.

"John . . . *John!*" Peg lightly slapped his cheeks. For a second, he slipped back into focus.

"Peg?" he whispered, looked around. "Oh, my God!"

The walls regained some substance, but still weren't solid. Grand Central Station stood around them in a sort of ghostly translucence.

"We've got to get out of here," Peg said, her face close to John's. "You need a doctor—a hospital."

John's face took on a faraway look that Harry now recognized. He was monitoring the state of the Rift.

"Can't get back to Earth," John murmured. "The currents are against us."

"Well, we can't hang around here much longer," Harry said. "Where *can* we go?" For a second, he thought of the world of the cloud-scraping towers. Now *that* would be a destination!

John's face, however, was uneasy beneath his pain. "Closest I can reach is the world the giants came from."

"Then I hope they've got good doctors there, because that's where we've got to go."

John closed his eyes, and most of the station around them rippled out of existence.

"John!" Peg cried in panic.

"Hold tight—here we go." John's wan voice was the only warning they got before the Rift closed in again. Harry found himself enduring an even worse trip than the last. Transiting the Rift was at best like trying the parachute jump at Coney Island. This was more like taking a ride on a corkscrew roller coaster.

Harry became aware of a low cry—was he hearing it through the void or was the vibration making itself felt through his death grip on John and Peg?

One thing was certain—it meant trouble. Their movement became more erratic. They seemed to pinwheel through oblivion, bereft of any sense of direction.

The kid's lost it, Harry thought. We're out of control. We'll spin on and on forever.

Yammering panic beat at his brain as he tried to wrestle with this concept. Harry's head ached, the kind of pain he usually associated with straining muscles unused to work. His fingers clenched harder around John's and Peg's wrists.

Gotta stop this, Sturdley thought. *Got to!*

A deep, wrenching sensation tore through every cell of his body.

Then Harry was tumbling free, alone.

It took him an instant to realize he was in shadow, rather than the endless dark of the Rift.

Then he hit solid ground—actually, yielding soil deeply covered in fallen leaves, much to his relief.

Harry lay winded, too nerveless to move. One fact

penetrated, though. The air he was drawing into his starved lungs was chilly—in fact, downright cold.

Forcing himself into motion, Harry sat up against the damp earth. First things first. "Peg!" he called, his voice quickly absorbed by the heavy tree trunks around him.

Sturdley cupped his hands around his mouth, calling again. "Hey, *Peg!*"

Oddly, he felt convinced he knew which direction she was in. Peg was south of him, although he didn't know how far away. Harry yelled twice more, until his voice was cracking.

Okay. If she were in that direction, she was apparently beyond earshot. What about John?

Instantly, Harry got a similar impression of location. Except John was some indefinite distance to the *north.*

Unhappily, Harry sucked in air between his teeth. What John Cameron needed most right now was an emergency room and intensive care. What he'd probably gotten instead was a crash landing into a tree. And the only one of them who knew anything about first aid was farther away from John than Sturdley.

Harry rose to his feet and headed south. That undefinable sensation in the back of his brain told him that Peg was closer and in some kind of trouble. What he sensed of John, on the other hand, seemed to indicate that he was in stable condition somewhere to the north.

Sturdley set off at as good a pace as he could manage, moving among the trees. He walked in a shadowy gloom, the sunlight barely making its way through the canopy of greenery far overhead.

This was ancient forest, with trees that had been here for centuries, their trunks large enough to hollow out and use as condominiums. There were a lot of conifers, and drawing on cloudy memories of Boy Scout training, Harry managed to identify something that looked like an oak leaf, some maples, and a large number of elms.

One major difference between wherever he was and San Diego came to him whenever he drew a breath. Besides being chilly, the air had a curious metallic tang. It wasn't just the lack of pollutants—this was simply . . . alien.

Sturdley shook his head. Speculation was fine in its place, but what he needed right now was hard facts—facts and his companions back. He continued on his southward route.

At least with an ancient forest, there were only trees to deal with—any underbrush had been killed for lack of light. That left Sturdley with a clear course to chart. The only drawbacks were the ground fog and the soggy humus he had to travel through. Harry had chosen comfortable walking shoes for his day at the convention, but the soft leather loafers were not up to a cross-country hike. His feet were soon squishing, and he suspected he was growing a blister on his left heel. The damp spots on his back and butt where he'd rested against the soggy mulch weren't going away, and the air still seemed cold against his perspiring skin.

He felt like a ghost wafting through a huge, randomly columned cathedral, that impression only strengthened by the ground mist rising up among the tree trunks.

In the distance, Sturdley got the impression of stronger sunlight. He aimed for the break in the canopy almost eagerly. For one thing, it might tell him where he was—or wasn't. If old familiar Sol wasn't high in the sky, he'd know he wasn't on Earth anymore.

The clearing had been formed by the fall of one of the giants of the forests. Its crash had torn a great swath through the greenery.

The opening to the sky had also allowed undergrowth to gain a root-hold—thorny bushes, mainly. Before Sturdley reached the clearing, his arms were scratched, his trousers torn, and his clothes covered with stickleberry twigs until he looked like a camouflaged commando.

Slapping at mosquitoes and no-see-ems, Sturdley finally got a decent view of the heavens—an anticlimax, really. The sky was a familiar murky blue, and the sun indistinguishable from the one that usually shone down on New York City.

"Well, that was a big waste of time," Harry muttered, swatting away at persistent insect life.

Beyond the clearing, the ancient growth thinned out. Either there'd been a fire, or this area had been cleared by humans in the last few generations. The second growth was lower and considerably more tangled with brush. Sturdley found himself threading a complicated course to avoid the worse thickets, although the strange internal compass he'd picked up on arrival here always told him which direction led to Peg.

Harry gingerly shoved aside some branches of stickleberry to find . . . empty ground.

He pushed through, gaining a couple of more twigs as decoration, then dropped to one knee and scuffed his hand across the naked dirt. The soil was a little soggy, but its center had been trodden down until it was harder than the edges. Sturdley pushed down a rush of irrational elation. *It's not as though this is a paved road,* he told himself. *It could be a game trail.*

At least it headed in the direction he wanted to go.

As Harry followed the dirt track, he noticed how it wound between trees, always following the path of least resistance around any hills. His spirits sank. That did seem to indicate an animal trail.

After about half an hour's travel, he came upon a small creek. The ground was mushier than usual, so he had to watch his step.

Then he saw it, on the far bank of the stream—a single footprint. Feeling like Robinson Crusoe, Sturdley stepped across the water and bent over the single track. It was human scale, somewhat smaller than the dimensions of Harry's size twelve loafer. Then Harry realized something else. There were no toeprints. Whoever had left that imprint had been wearing a foot covering of some kind.

Sturdley increased his pace. Somewhere at the other end of this path there had to be people. That meant food, shelter, and perhaps assistance in finding Peg and John. The day was waning, and the air was rapidly growing cooler. Harry beat his arms against his sides, thinking about warmth, company, and help.

Sturdley became so involved in planning what to do when he eventually met the natives of this world that he was unprepared for the reality.

From behind him came a wild, raucous cry, then the pounding of feet on the trail.

For an instant, Harry froze in midstride, almost overwhelmed as the very air seemed to radiate hate at him. Then he realized that the wave of hostility flooding his mind came from a small party of humans rapidly closing in from behind. He took off at a run down the forest path.

So much for help, Sturdley thought, trying to ignore the sudden stitch in his side. These guys broadcast hatred better than that neo-Nazi guy on cable TV. They ran after him, yelling and screaming. The path snaked and curved so much, he couldn't get a clear view of his pursuers, which he decided was a good thing. If they were armed, they wouldn't be able to get a clear shot at him.

However, as he dashed along, a new and disturbing thought came to Harry's mind. If this path belonged to the people who were pounding after him, it probably led to their hometown, or village, or whatever.

Now, a worried voice asked in the back of his brain, if the guys behind are hostile, what do you think your reception will be from anybody you meet in front?

Sturdley saw a break in the underbrush that lined the path and dove through it. Leaving the trail made for much slower going. Low-hanging branches lashed at his face, and he had to veer wildly to avoid thickets of heavier growth. Without his new-found inner compass, he'd have been lost in moments.

But he hadn't lost his pursuers. They had simply burst through the brush, baying like a pack of hunting hounds. Sturdley's lead melted away step by step.

Harry found himself staggering up a hill, chivvied onward by his pursuers. From the summit, he glanced back to see the pack of hunters fanning out behind him. Harry drew ragged breaths, his lungs feeling as if he was inhaling thousands of tiny needles. He saw there was no hope of doubling back, or veering off to outflank the pack.

In fact, he realized as he stumbled down the slope, if the flankers got ahead of him, they could inexorably close the circle and leave him surrounded.

Sturdley pushed himself onward with a spurt of pure panic. He plunged to the bottom of the hillside, immediately blundering into a marshy spot. "Shit," he muttered through clenching teeth, nearly losing a loafer as he pulled free a bogged-down foot.

He was now in the center of a crescent of hunters who communicated among one another with hoots and screeches. Slogging along as best he could, Harry only got occasional glimpses of dark-clad figures jogging relentlessly behind him, or dashing past him to the sides.

As Sturdley watched the bushes to his right, an exposed root caught his foot and Harry flopped flat on his face.

He pushed himself up, running a quick mental assessment. The wind had been knocked out of him, and his foot would doubtless sport a significant bruise. But nothing was broken. A triumphant yell from behind galvanized him into movement. The best pace Sturdley was able to maintain now was something between a skip and a hop. I'm dead meat, he thought grimly.

As if to underscore that notion, cries now came from ahead of him. Nowhere to run, and I'm seriously outnumbered. Not to mention that the only kind of combat I'm trained for is political infighting at editorial meetings.

Harry glanced down at the loosely fitting rags that once had been a casually elegant sports ensemble, and a grin crossed his face. I've always said the tighter the costume, the stronger the hero. In this getup, I look—and feel—like a ninety-eight-pound weakling.

He lurched to the largest-size tree in sight and put his back to the trunk. The rough bark rasped against his skin through the ruins of his lightweight summer shirt. Sturdley didn't brace himself against the tree merely for defensive reasons. His legs were barely able to keep him upright.

The underbrush all around him rustled with the approach of his pursuers. Men came bursting through the bushes—most of them barely came up to Sturdley's shoulders. They were hunched, rawboned, wild-eyed, their faces tight as they aimed crude spears at Sturdley's stomach. At second glance, Sturdley saw the roughly sewn hide and fur clothing, the half-starved looks on the hunters' faces.

The largest of the hunters spoke, a deep, guttural language that Sturdley had never heard in his life.

But somehow, Harry understand the words as if their meaning was being directly transmitted to his brain.

The leader looked him up and down. "Too old, skinny, nothing of value on him." He leaned on his spear, gesturing to the others. "Might as well kill him now and be done with it."

CHAPTER 11

When Peg Faber was growing up, a rebellious tomboy with wild red hair, her parents had taken her every year to the county fair. She'd been fascinated by the animals and delighted with the tests of skill, winning a menagerie of stuffed animals at the ball-toss and the shooting gallery.

But she hated any rides involving more motion than the merry-go-round. Inevitably, the fair always boasted something called the Whip, or the Do-se-do, or the Screwball, designed to whirl people around until they barfed. Someone would always talk her onto the long line to ride one of these centrifugal torture devices, and she'd go because she didn't want her friends thinking she was chicken.

Well, I still hate them and I'm still chicken, Peg thought as she, John, and Harry Sturdley endured the gyrations of an uncontrolled transit through the Rift. The drop into nothingness was usually no picnic, but this whip-sawing tumble felt like a speeded-up version of what Dorothy and Toto must have endured when the twister sucked them up. And Peg had the bad feeling that she would end up far from Kansas, too.

She clung desperately to John, doing her best to keep his wound closed. We've asked too much of him, she thought in dull horror. Maybe we've killed him.

Then came the jolting wrench, and Peg was in normal space, feeling as if she'd been spit out of a giant mouth. She landed hard on some kind of strawlike stubble growing out of loamy soil. The impact left her breathless, half-conscious, and lying on her side.

Peg drew a long, shuddering breath, wincing at the pain in her ribs, and pushing herself upright. She was still a little hazy until she looked down at her right hand and saw the bloody feminine napkin she still clutched. That sight brought her right to her feet, crying for John. With no one to stanch the flow of blood, his life would simply leak away. She took an instinctive step toward the north, to where John was, then halted, irresolute.

How did she know he was in that direction?

A more chilling question hit her. How was she so certain he was far away? Peg put her hands to her head, massaging her temples. A faint buzzing filled her skull. Maybe I landed harder than I thought. Could this be a concussion? She closed one eye, then the other. Everything seemed in focus.

Peg felt an urge to run like mad across the fields. If she were right about John being far away, she'd never find him in time to help. She'd known his condition was critical. If he had landed out in the middle of nowhere as she did, he'd been condemned to death.

Peg choked back tears and forced herself to take stock.

She was standing in the midst of flatlands, a vast rolling plain, overstretched by a bleak sky with a watery, diminished sun. The farther distance was walled off by woods. Her landing spot was a recently harvested field, filled with raggedly chopped stubble only beginning to dry out into straw.

Between her and the woods stood fields of still-ripening grain, some sort of barley, she thought. It was a pretty puny crop, the stalks stunted and crooked, bending their heads toward the ground, giving the fields a depressingly mangy appearance.

Peg had grown up in the mountains of Pennsylvania, in a college town, but there were plenty of hard-scrabble farms in the surrounding countryside. She knew what a farm looked like—even a poor one. And the struggling hillside fields she remembered looked downright prosperous next to this.

The soil was definitely fertile and well-watered. It was sticking to one side of her. Peg rubbed crumbs of dirt of her left arm and leg. A disturbing thought occurred. With soil this rich, even last century's farming technology would have yielded a far more abundant harvest.

Instead, Peg felt oppressed by a sense of poverty and . . . primitiveness. The grain looked as if it had been sown by someone poking a stick in to the ground and scattering seeds around. The stubble that surrounded her also suggested that the harvest had been done by people hacking away with sickles.

"This sure as hell *ain't* Kansas," she muttered. And if the local level of agriculture was any indication, the only medical help she could get for John would come in the form of a witch doctor.

Peg started off to the north again, unsure why she should head in that direction, but bolstered by a weird, intuitive feeling that this was the way that led to Harry and John. Harry somehow felt nearer. Maybe she could link up with him.

She rubbed her arms as she walked, her skin crawling with gooseflesh. Peg managed a crooked grin as she looked down at herself, inadequately protected from the chill air by a sleeveless jersey T-shirt. Damn, it's so cold. Got to get warm, get something to cover myself, find Harry . . .

She stumbled to a halt, shaking her head. The buzzing between her ears grew louder.

What the hell is wrong with me? she thought. Her heart was pounding in her chest with a sudden unknown dread. All her consciousness seemed to shudder under a barrage of alien thoughts—hostility, avarice, raw *lust.*

The unmown grain rustled apart and three men pushed through into the clearing. Peg's physical senses told her they were sweaty, dirty, and coarsely clad.

But her brain reeled from the impact of their thoughts. Graphic images of rape and degradation bombarded her. She was just a Breeder, better-looking than most, not as worn as the others they'd enjoyed. They'd enjoy her, too, then seek a profit. Peg saw her favors being pimped to a faceless horde of customers—"favors,' hell. She saw her every bodily orifice rented out for a handful of grain or a dead chicken. And when she was worn out, she'd be discarded. All of this struck her the moment her mind touched theirs.

Peg drew breath in short, panting gasps, a band of pain running round her head as she struggled to process the blitz of images.

She blinked, feeling as if she had just lived through weeks. But it had barely been seconds. The trio of would-be rapists was now halfway across the field and closing in on her.

There was no time for considered thought. Peg ran like a deer. She'd never been track-team material, but her sprint was impressive. The three stooges pursuing her were caught flat-footed for an instant, then upped their pace with guttural cries.

For a moment or two Peg put some distance between herself and the pack. Unfortunately, the three men behind her were skilled in running down prey. The safety of the woods, the only hiding place in sight, was still half a mile off when a pair of hairy arms were flung round her legs in a jarring tackle.

Peg hit the ground with numbing force, but she was paralyzed more by the thoughts spewing through her brain. The physical contact enhanced her new-found mental reception. She was feeling everything he intended to do before he made a move. The very air she breathed seemed overly warm, thick, and musky as he grabbed an ankle, flipping Peg onto her back.

A demonic grin showed snaggleteeth among a bristling, unkempt beard tangled with food. A rank odor emanated from the shapeless, burlaplike clothing the man wore, and his breath was foul. A filthy hand with grime-encrusted cracked fingernails seized the neck of her T-shirt, tearing at it. The cloth burned into her neck, then gave, tearing in two. He grabbed her right breast in its light sports bra, giggling to himself. And throughout it all, images slammed into her mind of this animal plowing her, grinding her into the dirt under his body while his pals waited for their turn. The crashing horror of it seemed to turn her muscles into putty.

But as he wrangled her body around, trying to tear her bra loose, fury exploded like a nova in her brain. It pushed away the battering mind-pictures. For a second, everything became crystal-clear. She heard the quiet voice of her martial arts instructor: *"Focus."*

Peg focused her energy, then snapped a kick right up

between her attacker's legs. He tumbled back, clutching himself with a howl of pain as she lurched to her feet. There were still two more to be dealt with, and they were right on top of her.

She kept most of her attention on the larger of the two men, whose muscular shoulders strained the sacking material of the shirt and loose trousers he wore. He had dark, curly hair and regular features. Cleaned up, she might have enjoyed meeting him in more civilized circumstances. He also had an open countenance that now showed surprise and a little shock that she was resisting them.

His companion was a rusty-haired, skinny little runt whose lean and hungry features showed a familial resemblance to old Snaggletooth, who was still huddled in on himself, venting his pain.

The two remaining attackers split up, circling around her.

Peg felt a surge of irritation. I should have nailed one of them right away, while they were still surprised over what I'd done to their friend.

She retreated a couple of steps, angling to her left so the little guy was between her and his big partner. His lips lifted from crooked teeth, and he leapt for her, trying to grab her arm.

Damn, he's fast, Peg thought, leaping backward while still unleashing a low kick at him. She had to strike off-balance, and her blow landed on his shin rather than the kneecap as she'd aimed. He yelled and hopped back. Double damn. If that kick had gone as planned, his kneecap would have popped out and he'd have been out of the fight.

The big guy moved to her right, feinting, and she had to backpedal and turn to meet him. Rusty the Runt was spitting incomprehensible curse words and testing his weight on his leg. He'd be back at her in a second.

But for the moment, she faced only the man-mountain. And if she could take him out, she had a chance. It would take split-second coordination—she couldn't be sloppy again. Bracing her right foot, Peg prepared to launch into a leaping high kick. If she caught the guy off-guard, she might actually hit him in the throat and put him down. Even if she only caught him in the chest, it should be enough to knock him down. She could either finish him with a hand blow, or take the fight to Rusty.

But before she leapt, a grip like iron clamped onto her right ankle.

These guys are tough, Peg thought as she was pulled to the ground. I thought that shot to the family jewels would keep him out of things for a while.

She tried to land as she'd learned at the dojo, slapping the ground and rolling to her feet. But Snaggletooth was trying to twine himself around her. She writhed in an attempt to twist free, aiming a blow for his midsection.

His fist smashed into the left side of her head.

The world darkened and seemed to swirl away as the man forced her body prone again. Operating on sheer instinct, she tried to smash the heel of her hand into his nose.

This time she was rocked by a blow to her right temple, a kick from Rusty the Runt. She was barely aware of the big man grabbing the little guy's elbow, arguing. Probably complaining about him damaging the merchandise, Peg thought groggily.

She tried to will resistance back into sluggish muscles as the runt yanked up her bra and his snaggle-toothed brother wrestled with the waistband of her shorts. The little guy yelled something impatiently to the man-mountain. He moved to grab her wrists and pin them above her head.

With his hands on her, the stereo telepathic show of what would happen to her, provided by the snaggle brothers, became a three-way affair. Thoughts she never would have entertained in her darkest fantasies squirmed through her mind. She screamed, involuntarily recoiling as she tried to push the thoughts away.

Peg's face contorted into a mask of ferocity, teeth bared in a snarl, tendons pulling every plane of flesh taut, her eyes wide but unseeing. Rage, fear, and corrosive fury blared from her mind.

She lay back in the dirt, panting, her very brain feeling spent, the mother of all headaches throbbing along her nerves, a vaguely sick feeling in the pit of her stomach. Then she realized the hands had stopped moving over her body.

As her eyes finally refocused, Peg found her three assailants frozen. Snaggletooth and the runt had actually drawn back, while the big guy knelt over her, his hands still on her wrists, his handsome features hanging slackly.

Snaggletooth bared his twisted dentition, superstitious dread warring with lust. His clawed fingers moved back to her shorts.

Peg glared into the empty eyes of the man-mountain, her thoughts flowing through the connection between her wrists and his fingers.

Don't just kneel there, she blazed at him, *do something!*

As if in a trance, he released her wrists, turned, and slugged the runt.

Snaggletooth stared openmouthed, and Peg took advantage of his distraction to arch free of him. She rose to one knee and cocked her arm in one motion. This time when she struck, the heel of her palm connected perfectly. The cartilage of Snaggletooth's nose splintered under the blow, and he flopped back, his face a bloody ruin.

Before he even hit the ground, she followed up that punch with a hammer-blow to the side of his head. Rapist number one was out for the count.

Peg turned to the struggle going on beside her. In spite of the difference in size between the two combatants, the runt was getting the upper hand. The big guy she'd sicced on him was moving in slow motion. His rusty-haired enemy kicked him in the face, jolting him back. Man-mountain lay panting, blood coursing down from the side of his lip.

Snarling, the little guy glanced at Peg, gauging whether he could get to her before his erstwhile comrade could get up.

Peg made it easy for him, coming straight at the runt. She aimed a flurry of karate kicks and chops at the guy, driving him back in surprise.

Grab him, she beamed at her large ally.

The big guy flung out an arm, tripping the rusty-haired runt. Peg finished him off with a knee to the gut and an elbow to the temple.

Two down, she thought, drawing herself into the defensive position that Master Hisoka had taught her. The big guy was coming out of his trance. He gawked at the two others lying on the ground. And the look he directed at her didn't bode well.

Wiping blood from his lips with the back of a hairy hand, he lunged at her. For a big guy, he was remarkably agile. Peg tried to dodge aside, but a huge arm caught her, drew her in, and the big man brought her to the ground.

She *oofed* as his weight landed atop her.

Peg cupped her hands and slammed them to either side of his head, just over the ears. The big man reared back, but his arm tightened around her. There'd be no escape this time. His right hand came up and clamped onto her left wrist, yanking her hand away before she could claw him. Peg resisted with every fiber in her body, but it was like being caught in a steel vise.

His other hand was coming for her free wrist. She had to do something. Plastering her hand to his temple, she exercised those brain circuits she never knew she'd had.

Hold still.

The grabbing hand slowed, then stopped only inches from her wrist. He lay heavily atop her, dead weight. Peg tried to extricate her captured wrist, twisting against slightly slackened fingers. It was as if the movement brought him back to life—or maybe it was the break in her own concentration. His grip on her wrist tightened, and his other hand closed.

Their connection became a two-way street, with pictures of what he intended to do broadcasting themselves in the back of her brain. His mental porn show wasn't quite as degrading as his friends', but still a shudder of disgust run through her.

No! she sent the thought stabbing into his brain. *Stop!*

The big man's eyes rolled up and his breath rattled in his throat. Back arching, his hamlike hands released her wrists. Peg rolled out from under him as he fell on his back.

He'd taken her mental command a bit too literally, she realized, putting a hand to his chest. No heartbeat, no respiration.

"Ohmigod," Peg muttered. "I killed him!" She

glanced at the three still forms. "And he's the one who deserved it least."

She took the man's head in her hands and reopened the connection. *Heart, start beating. Lungs, start breathing. Everything start working again.*

The big man drew a deep, convulsive breath.

Peg let her consciousness expand along the linkage between them. She was touching the upper emotions of his unconscious mind.

Yes, the guy was big, but he wasn't a bully. He was easygoing, maybe too easily led . . .

Peg suddenly found herself thinking of John Cameron.

Wake up, she transmitted along the link.

His eyes blinked open, staring up at her.

"You've got to have a name," Peg muttered. Removing one hand from his head, she tapped his chest.

Who? she sent.

"M-Maahkh," he said, licking his lips.

The answer came more clearly through their linkage. *Mike.*

"Okay, Mike," Peg told him. "I need help, and you're going to help me."

She rammed that idea hard into his consciousness watching him wince. *Help me, right?*

Mike nodded. *Yes.*

Peg didn't know if that answer came from him, or if it was only an echo of what she'd implanted. Right now, she couldn't worry about that.

She rose to her feet, pulling her clothing together. That only made her more aware of the chill in the air.

Face set in distaste, she went to the prone figure of the runt. I hope to God he doesn't have too many fleas, she thought as she began undoing his clothing. But beggars can't be choosers.

CHAPTER 12

Tree bark gouged Harry Sturdley's back as he instinctively tried to thrust himself away from the spears raised to skewer him. His eyes squeezed shut to close off his imminent demise, but his mind's eye nevertheless painted the scene all too clearly. *No! Stop! Hold it!* Desperate commands blared in his brain, a denial of death fueled by shock and sheer terror.

Wish fulfillment, of course, another side of Harry's mind commented sardonically. But no spears pierced his flesh. It's like that movie short I saw years ago, the one where the guy has an entire adventure in his head during the moment it takes for him to drop to the end of the hangman's rope. I'll open my eyes just in time to see myself get stabbed.

The moment seemed to drag out forever, the only reality the rasp of the corrugated tree trunk against Harry's skin. Finally, he couldn't stand it anymore, and opened his lids. His attackers still stood around him in threatening poses . . . but they seemed frozen in place.

Sturdley stepped away from the tree, surveying the tableau around him. It looked like a display from the Museum of Natural History, a spear-carrying group of men and women in roughly sewn clothes that would have borne a placard reading "A hunting party of the Kakkalakka tribe."

But these hunters weren't models made of wax and wood, dressed with props. A faint constriction across his temples, a low-pitched buzzing in his ears, a feeling of unconscious effort now become conscious—Harry realized *he* was the one holding these people motionless through the power of his mind. The tribesfolk seemed to realize it, too. Although they couldn't move, terror shone bright in their eyes.

Incredible, Harry thought. This must be like what Madam Vile is able to do to her enemies. No, it's *stronger*. She can only hit them with horrible, disgusting thoughts. I'm actually holding these people prisoner with mental energy. *There's* a superpower for you—and a great new character. Mastermind? No, *Mindmaster!* Marty Burke thinks he's such hot shit with Mr. Pain. Wait till he sees the stories I can write for Mindmaster—because I'll know his powers from the inside out!

Reality reasserted itself. He'd never write comics again unless he managed to return to Earth. That wouldn't happen unless he found John Cameron. Could he use his newfound mental powers to reach the kid's mind?

Sturdley made the attempt, straining his new mental muscles.

No contact. But the chief in front of Harry shuddered into movement for a second, taking a step closer, raising his spear.

Sturdley dropped his long-range scan, popping back to the here-and-now. He froze the chieftain of this hunting party, then forced the men on either side of him to turn to their erstwhile leader, threatening him with their weapons.

"Maybe *that* will teach you to be a wise guy," Harry said. "Don't you realize you're up against something that can't be fought with a spear?"

Right, he thought. I'm invulnerable, as long as I can keep up this standoff. But if I get distracted, he'll put three feet of sharpened tree-branch into my gut.

A worse thought hit him. What happens when I fall asleep? The magic wears off, and again, I get a new belly button courtesy of the chief here.

Harry frowned. Maybe I could hold them in check till I put enough distance between us.

He looked at the chieftain's face. Would he have been scared enough by then to take his people away from the bad ju-ju? Or would the hunt merely begin again? Sturdley did not want to spend his days and nights on this world looking over one shoulder.

That left a single, grisly alternative. He could kill them—hold them all entranced and slit their helpless throats. Only problem was, he didn't even have a pocketknife to do the job.

Well, he could borrow the chief's spear.

It was an unpalatable choice. Sturdley only wrote about mayhem; he hadn't actually participated in any except for that brief stint in Korea. He cast about desperately for some other way out.

They stood absolutely silent, a Paleolithic still life, until something snorted off in the underbrush, and Harry discerned a possible out.

Carefully, he extended a psychic probe in the direction of the snort. Yes. A big beast with horns. Deer? Moose? Elk? He couldn't tell. The point was that it could feed this tribe for a week.

Come here, Sturdley transmitted to the animal. *Right this way. There's a big female horny beast, waiting just for you.*

Another snort rang out, and the bushes began to shake. This wasn't easy. Harry felt like a kid again, back at his grammar school show, juggling the Indian clubs. Except he had too many in the air, keeping the chief and his people still, drawing in this animal . . .

The two hunters he'd turned on the chief slowly turned back to face Sturdley. They seemed to be moving through glue, but they were definitely moving. The chief's spear arm went back for a throw. *Come on, beastie,* Harry sent. *What's keeping you?* Sweat beaded on his forehead, running down his face.

The greenery behind Harry rustled apart and the animal crashed through. Finding itself nose-to-nose with a bunch of humans, catching their scent, galvanized it into action.

With a trumpeting cry, the beast half-turned to plunge back into the deeper forest. But it couldn't. Harry reached out psychically to snare its muscles. The animal shuddered to a stop.

The humans, however, completely burst their mental fetters as Harry gratefully released them.

Shouting at the top of his lungs, the chief flung his spear. It caught the horned beast in its shaggy side. Resistance flared against Harry's mental bonds, but he held them tight. The other hunters moved in against the strangely quiet prey, stabbing with their weapons. The crude spears thudded home into the beast's flesh with disgustingly resilient sounds. Blood spattered as they stabbed again and again.

As one man rammed his spear into the animal's

brain through an eye socket, Harry released his control and the horned creature collapsed.

The tribespeople immediately set to work skinning the animal and butchering it, a damned messy job with the primitive tools they had at hand.

Harry stepped around to confront the chief, who was pulling his spear from the creature's flank. The man brought his weapon down in readiness.

With his left hand, Harry made a dismissive gesture. His right hand tapped his chest, then pointed to the dead animal. *I brought this beast here,* he sent to the chief. *Me!*

The chief looked puzzled, but gestured from the animal to Harry. Obviously, words wouldn't quite do the job. So Harry visualized a picture, he and the chief sitting together with the whole tribe, the carcass of the beast roasting over a fire, as they feasted. A succession of horned beasts marched one behind the other into the spears of the tribesmen.

"Get it now?" Harry asked the chief. "I've just appointed myself Wise Old Man of this tribe. Do what I say and you'll have full bellies all the time."

The meaning of the images got through if not the words. The chief grinned, showing discolored teeth behind his shaggy beard as he nodded. He touched his chest. "Aahl," he said.

"Pleased to meet you, Al," Harry said. "You can call me—" He grinned for a moment, remembering a line from the Sherlock Holmes stories he'd loved as a youth. "You can call me The Great Lord Harry." He thumped his chest and repeated his self-awarded title.

Al nodded. "Graylaw Horry," he echoed.

* * *

The elklike meat had gone down pretty well, flame-broiled on a spit with some sort of herbs added while the meat turned. Kind of on the gamy side, but Harry was used enough to that: One of the more countrified O'Fanahan cousins, part of the far-flung stockholder clans who owned the Fantasy Factory, fancied himself another Rambo. Every hunting season brought the Sturdleys venison steaks.

Chewing the last of his meal, Harry looked over the tribe he'd fallen in with—tribelet, really. Maybe *clan* was a better description. Seen at leisure rather than glanced over his shoulder while he ran like a stag, Harry saw there were fewer than a dozen of them: four men including Al, the chief, three women, and a gaggle of children ranging from a baby in arms to an adolescent boy.

Harry could see that life was hard for them. Beyond the crude clothing and spears, he'd already spotted a long, puckered scar running down from Al's chest to disappear under the fur jerkin he wore. The tribesfolk wore moccasins, but most of the furs they wore were raw and stinking. As he watched the women bank the fire and prepare to smoke the leftover meat, he realized they could be any age between twenty and fifty. Exposure and deprivation had molded their faces into ageless—or rather, prematurely aged—masks.

Turning to Al, Harry decided the time had come to play anthropologist. He had to understand how this society functioned to see where his Wise Old Man act would work best. Obviously, bringing the stag in for the slaughter had been a big hit. These people lived by the hunt, judging from the way the whole tribe had fallen in to chase him through the forest. Were they only hunters and gatherers?

Harry projected an image to Al, of the tribe marching through the woods, the men breaking off to chase a deer.

Al nodded his head in a decided affirmative, snatching up his spear as if he thought another deer were about to walk into camp. Harry calmed him down, showing more pictures: the women and children gathering nuts, berries, and herbs; the men teaching the boys to hunt.

Again he was met with an affirmative rumble from Al. That was their life.

Tentatively, Harry projected a picture of Al behind a plow, with the tribe sowing grain. Behind them walked a cow and some chickens.

Al's negative response was just as strong as his previous "yes" answers. Harry wasn't exactly surprised. Hunters often didn't get along with agricultural societies. What interested him, though, was that Al's response had been one of fear, rather than dislike or disdain.

Now Harry tried a projection of Al standing outside a house, a simple log cabin. He tried to add a question. *Why don't you live in one place?*

Al got more agitated, closing his eyes and changing the picture. He showed a giant foot coming into the picture, kicking in the walls of the cabin, crushing the crops, stomping on the pig—finally stomping on the image of Al.

For a long moment, Harry looked at the chief of this woods clan in silence. Obviously, Al had very little use for Robert's kind.

He created a new picture—Al standing next to a hero—although he kept off the costume his artists had invented and dressed the giant in what he knew to be their traditional style—something in between a jock-strap and swaddling clothes.

Harry projected the image, adding a querying tone.

Again, Al changed the picture. He still came up only to the giant's knee, but he was dressed differently, in a heavy shirt and trousers of some kind of homespun material. Al also didn't just stand there; he cowered as the giant made commanding and threatening gestures. Al joined many humans, similarly clad, trailing behind the giant, working in fields, fighting with other giants' servants. Not the most pleasant lifestyle. Finally the Al image ran away into the forest. His homespun clothes turned to the crude and shaggy jerkin and leggings the chief now wore, and his cowering attitude changed to one of leadership.

Clear enough, Harry thought. The home life of the heroes wasn't exactly heroic, while life for the humans on this world was more like serfdom. Al had run away to breathe free.

What was life like for the people of the forest? Harry thought for a moment before offering another vision to Al. He showed Al's tribelet meeting other clans, other chieftains.

Al took the picture and immediately darkened it. Spears flew. Men died. Because Al and his people were the heroes of the chief's mind, they won the skirmish, taking women and binding captives. The coffle of prisoners was marched toward smock-clad men in the distance. Farther beyond them, well away from the action, a giant rose.

Sturdley's face tightened into planes and angles. *Slavery.* There was a lot about this world Robert hadn't mentioned. He re-created his all-purpose giant image.

Attached to it, he projected a query. The giant tapped its chest. *What name?*

Al stared at Harry as if surprised he didn't know. "Maazdah," he answered aloud.

His mental response came through much more clearly.

Master.

Peg Faber and her new companion, Mike, crouched behind the cover of a shed—more like a log lean-to—as figures passed by the boundary of one of the unharvested fields. As she knelt, she slipped a hand inside the smock that billowed around her frame and scratched vigorously. It was as she feared. The clothing that had belonged to Rusty the randy runt was also inhabited by the local version of fleas. She sincerely hoped the bastard didn't have crabs, too.

Maybe if she boiled the rough-textured homespun—but that would mean dealing with more of the local population, and she wasn't sure she was up to that.

Unless . . . maybe her newfound powers could do the trick. She remembered an old horror novel she'd read, where Dracula psychically drove away a bunch of fleas. The question was, how to do it?

Peg tried to reach down to the tiny little bug-minds, broadcasting an order. *Buzz off!*

A heavy hand landed on her shoulder and attempted to yank off the smock. Mike was out of restraint, and obviously in an amorous mood.

Damn, Peg thought, I must have diverted too much juice to the bugs.

She gave Mike the old one-two—an elbow to the gut and a paralyzing psychic attack. Only after he'd folded to the ground did her hands begin to tremble in reaction. A dull ache throbbed in her temples.

An instant's inattention, and he'd been all over her. This would be a continuous drain unless she got rid of handsome here, or did him in. The problem was, she needed a guide to get across this bizarre landscape. Her first brush with the locals had nearly resulted in gang rape. On this world, ignorance meant death.

So Mike was necessary, but too dangerous in his present mindset. And she couldn't even *speak* to him. Their only communication had been when she'd gotten inside his head.

The phrase echoed in her mind. She'd been inside his head. Why not rearrange the furniture in there?

She yanked Mike upright, staring deep into his dark brown eyes. Let's hope those psych courses I took in college were good for something, she thought.

She probed into Mike's mind, scouting his upper thoughts. He wasn't vicious really, just burdened with some really rough edges.

She was suddenly overwhelmed by an image of herself, naked, straining under his nude body as they hammered together in a staccato, age-old rhythm.

In your dreams, cowboy! Peg's fingers clawed into pressure points on Mike's shoulders, but the pain she broadcast directly into his brain left him muscle-tensed and gasping.

Of course, the image *was* in his dreams, she realized. At least he had to decency to fantasize that I was enjoying myself, too, Peg thought wryly.

She returned to her probing. The porn loop with herself in the starring role was no longer in Mike's upper thoughts. She replayed an instant of it and felt him flinch.

Peg plunged deeper into his mind, hitting a seam of memories that brought a blush to her cheeks. Mike might be about her age, but he had considerably more sexual experience. Feeling like a voyeur, she examined his previous partners, finding most of them to be—well, trulls, *skanks* in more up-to-date parlance.

The college in her hometown had a thriving branch of the Society for Creative Anachronism, where students attempted to re-create the Middle Ages at meetings and fairs. Now Peg was seeing the reality of those buxom farm wenches, and it was far from the romantic fantasy of the SCA. They were coarse, hardened, tired and dirty, old before their time—the pretty ones quickly worn by male demand. Peg was a little taken aback to discover that Mike considered her a raving beauty, already ensconced among his ideal women, two of them untouchable giantesses, the others a handful of women with powerful protectors, Lessers whose services were of importance to the Masters.

Lessers. Peg realized she had somehow picked up the concept from Mike's mind. He identified himself and all the other humans by that term, as servants of the giant Masters.

Sweet culture they've got here, Peg thought, pulling back her probes.

She considered the man's face before her, softened now as he looked at her. So, on one level, he'd already idealized her. He knew there was such a thing as love, although it was pretty rare in local experience, and the process could hardly be described as courtly.

It's a pretty shitty way to control someone, Peg thought, but right now it's the best I can cobble together.

Probing his mind once again, she proceeded to edit

Mike's memories, making him a hero who'd rescued her from his friends. She seeded his mind with images of his deferring to her, reinforcing the behavior with bursts of intense pleasure. She implanted images of awe. She made Mike fall in love with her, then proceeded to train him how to handle that feeling platonically.

Three months of the mating dance, condensed into half an hour, Peg thought. Now she released her psychic holds. How're you gonna react, Mikey-baby?

The two of them were still on their knees facing each other. Mike looked into her eyes, his pupils dilating, a goofy look coming over his face.

Oh, jeeze, Peg thought, all of a sudden he looks like John.

Mike gave her a sudden, sweet smile as she removed her hands. Then shouting in the distance broke the tableau. Mike scuttled to the edge of the shed, peeking around. Instantly, he pulled his head back, looking scared.

Peg went to look, and he tried to push her back. She took advantage of the contact to project a question to him. *What is it?*

His answer was an image of a pair of giants, surrounded by retinues of Lessers.

A question came to Peg, and she did her best to convey it to Mike. *If that's the way the giants—Masters—go around, where's your Master?*

Another picture—Mike and his two friends, running off into the night.

So where's your Master?

Mike shrugged, shaking his head. He gave her a blurry mental picture of a giant, which suddenly cleared up.

Peg gasped. She knew that face. Not so long ago, it had advanced on her with blood in its eye.

It was the angular face of Thomas, the bad-attitude "hero."

CHAPTER 13

Robert sat on the grassy floor of a pavilion erected on the lawn of Heroes' Manor, the warm Westchester sun beating down on the grounds beyond the tent's cover. The head hero was hardly at ease, however. His eyes were glued to the image on a forty-inch TV screen set up under the canvas roof.

A perfectly coiffed newscaster gave the update on the shocking attack and disappearances at the San Diego Comics Con. Robert's lips twisted. It was merely a rehash of the same muddled facts the networks had on hand three hours before. How could the Lessers watch these uninformative "news" updates?

The only reliable report he had of the events in California had come over the phone from Thomas, and he had been forced to be circumspect. At least Thomas had kept an eye on the targets of the attack. The table they'd dropped behind might have covered them from the news crews, but Thomas had seen them shimmer and disappear into the Rift. He was also sure that John Cameron had indeed been struck by at least one shot. And, from the guarded references Thomas made, Robert had deduced that Harry Sturdley at least suspected who was behind the attack.

His hands bunched into fists the size of human

heads. Gods below! The entire thrust of this enterprise had been to simplify the situation, to take Cameron's powers out of Sturdley's control. Instead, Sturdley had escaped with Cameron's assistance, linking the one threat to Robert's plans with his former closest collaborator. The combination could prove disastrous for Robert and his followers.

All now depended on too many imponderable factors. Did Sturdley know his erstwhile heroes were behind the attack? Even if the humans were sure of that, Robert still had reason to believe that Sturdley wouldn't move too publicly. The fate of his precious comics company was by now too much bound to the public image of the heroes.

What *would* the Lesser do? Attack his heroes individually? Try to trap them? With Cameron's help, isolated members of Robert's group could even be exiled with the help of the Rift. Hadn't the young one been able to bring all forty-nine of them away from their world in a single Rifting?

Robert snarled silently at the screen. Of course, they had been cooperating with Cameron then, every step of the way. He might not find a transition so easy if the subject resisted, both mentally and physically. If only they knew how close Cameron had to be to work his magic! Without knowledge, any counterplanning became a long exercise in what-if and maybe.

Looking at the situation dispassionately, Robert concluded he could do nothing until Sturdley and Cameron turned up again. He discounted the girl from the equation, except as possible leverage on the young man. After all, reaching for her had apparently been the cause of his stepping into the assassins' fire.

Robert's best hope was the wound. If it were serious

enough, perhaps Cameron had failed to get them through the Rift. Perhaps the two humans were drifting endlessly with a corpse. Alternatively, they may have reached safety on this world—or perhaps on some other—and were waiting for Cameron to heal before attempting some sort of response.

In a perfect universe, the humans would have landed on Robert's homeworld. He smiled without mirth. *That* was a place that knew what to do with troublesome Lessers!

But that was too much to hope for. At present, Robert was certain of only two things. First, there would be no pay for Carron on this botched assassination. Second, the heroes would patrol every inch of New York City to try and locate Sturdley and Cameron. If they could be found alone, perhaps they could be disposed of. But Robert doubted things would resolve themselves so easily.

"Robert."

Barbara stood at the entrance to the tent, a giant-size cellular phone in her hands. "It's for you—a Marty Burke."

"I'm glad we could meet—ah, Robert."

Burke craned his neck to get some sort of eye contact with the giant. Robert had set the meeting at a new city landmark—the promontory jutting into Central Park's pond where the giants had first set up camp after their arrival. It was a quiet enough spot, but it was also one that made the most of the difference in their statures.

Robert sat, still looking down at Burke, who felt more and more like a suppliant. "Your phone call raised a valid point." Robert smiled, lifting a thought from Burke's upper mind. "But it was not one that could be discussed over a wire. I prefer to do my negotiating face-to-face."

"For obvious reasons," Burke said, a little shaken by the casual display of telepathy. "Well, I won't deny that Harry Sturdley and I have had our run-ins. I want the Fantasy Factory. Right now, you and the other heroes are our most important assets. Sturdley dealt with you personally. But now that he's disappeared—"

"*You* want to step in." Smiling, Robert raised a hand to cut off a rush of self-justification. "I already understand your motives, and I leave them to you. The fact of the matter is, my companions and I still have need of a liaison with the Fantasy Factory and the human public at large."

A tool, he added silently, more easily used than Harry Sturdley—one who could destroy Sturdley's power base and render him harmless—one who is connected with the mass media.

Robert gave his most benevolent look to the childishly eager Lesser beneath him.

"Tell your company that in the future we will work through you."

The giant maintained his smile as the human rushed off. And you will work for *us*.

The sounds of turmoil from beyond the lean-to grew more intense—wild cries, groans, infuriated shouting. Peg Faber headed to the corner of the crude log construction, firmly pushing down Mike's arms when he raised them protectively.

She kept close to the wall though, using as much cover as she could.

There was a riot in progress at the far end of the

field. Well, maybe it was a little small for that. Call it an oversize gang fight. A good hundred figures were locked in battle, swirling around the central confrontation between the two giants.

The two huge antagonists were duking it out in surprisingly Marquis of Queensbury fashion, moving with the almost stately precision Peg connected with boxing at its most old-fashioned—fists up with a slight bobbing and weaving movement.

Farther down the social and height scale, the giants' followers fought in a considerably more rough-and-tumble manner. The mob around the giants' knees boiled as if the combatants there were moving in fast-forward. Some rolled on the ground, strangling and tearing at each other. Three roughnecks ganged up on a single enemy, battering at him with fists and feet, until their party was broken up by a partisan of the other side suddenly smashing in one of the kicker's heads with a club.

Above, the lighter-haired of the two giants managed to land a cruel blow to his antagonist's solar plexus. The other giant froze for a second, and the fair-haired Master clouted him upside the head. All fighting stopped for a moment as followers on both sides watched the unfortunate giant reel around, out on his feet. Then the behemoth crumpled, falling to the ground as dozens of Lessers hastily vacated the ground.

The stunned giant landed with enough force for Peg to feel the impact. An expectant hush filled the battlefield as the humans formed a ring around the two huge figures. The downed giant stirred, rising up creakily on one elbow. His fair-haired adversary stepped forward, fist raised in silent threat. To Peg's dojo-trained eyes, it seemed less a fighting move than a ritual.

Her guess was proven true when the darker-haired giant painfully got to his knees and prostrated himself beneath the victor's outstretched fist.

The fair-haired guy's adherents cheered as the defeated giant rose to take a place behind the victor. Then the humans broke up their ring to coalesce into a single mob following the new Master and his subordinate.

Grinning in triumph despite a bloody lip, the blond giant led his force into the as yet untouched fields. Sheaves of unharvested grain were trodden down in the wake of the war party.

Peg barely noted their passage. Her eyes were glued to the human figures, some writhing in pain, some horribly still, that the victory parade had left behind. Another detail caught her attention. Off to one side, two groups of women moved in single file, their hands tied behind their backs, with ropes knotted leash-fashion from neck to neck. They moved at the rear of the column, surrounded by a scattering of guards. As she watched, one of the men joined the two groups into one long coffle, prodding them onward through the crushed grainfield. Peg turned to Mike, grabbing his hand. *Is this the way things usually happen around here?* she projected.

Mike gave a negative head shake. He pointed deeper into the cleared plain. Beyond the two giants and their followers, Peg made out columns of smoke rising into the late-afternoon sky.

Zeroing in on those areas with her newfound mental powers, she detected single minds wallowing in corrosive hate—renegade Lessers torching granaries and workers' barracks. There was a feeling of hysteria in the air, as if all constraints were off. But it didn't have the safety-valve feeling of a Mardi Gras. This spoke of social breakdown—civil war.

As if she were seeing it from a satellite, Peg suddenly caught a glimpse of a larger-scale struggle going on deeper in the cleared territory. Regiment-size mobs clashed over barns and silos. A good two dozen giants served as officers, some of them stomping enemy Lessers, others engaging in the single combat ritual. Several of the human combatants waved bloody farm implements over their heads.

This was obviously a culture in chaos—not a good place to be hanging around. Peg pulled in her probes, removing her consciousness from the battle scene and returning to her body. Mike looked at her with concern.

"We've got to get out of here," she muttered, leaning against the shed and turning to the wall of forest so tantalizingly close. Obviously, that's where Mike and his fellow runaways had been heading.

But if escape were so easily had, why were all those Lessers—humans—clinging to their slavery with the giants? Something didn't add up here. Peg hoped that Mike could explain.

She projected an image of herself and Mike running from the shed toward the shelter of the woods. *Why not do it right now?* she asked.

Mike shook his head vehemently, changing the picture to show them sneaking toward the tree line in darkness.

Why? Peg sent.

Mike responded with a montage of pictures. He showed their running forms being surrounded by a score of Lesser slaves as a Master suddenly burst from the cover of the trees. Mike was beaten and subjected to some sort of mumbo-jumbo by the giant. Peg was tied and added to a small coffle of women—prizes for the brave soldiers.

The picture changed again. This time, Mike and Peg were set upon by a pair of figures who looked suspiciously like Mike's former associates, Snaggletooth and the runt. They bopped Mike on the head and proceeded to ravish Peg.

Mike shuddered at the thought, obviously repellent to him.

What a difference a brainwash makes, Peg thought.

Again, the image shifted. In this version, Mike and Peg made it into the woods, only to be attacked by what looked like cavemen in fur clothes and shaggy hair. This time Mike was killed while the savages took their pleasure with Peg.

Apparently, the cavemen got so distracted with their party that they never noticed the gang of Lessers moving in on them. This crew all carried clubs and was led by a giant who stepped onto the scene after the head breaking was over. Such savages as survived were roped into line. Peg was added to an already existing female coffle.

Great, she thought, equal opportunity imprisonment.

The pictures faded and Mike looked at her with a pleading expression.

He doesn't want to put me in harm's way, Peg realized. "Let's see if I've got this straight. We've got to worry about Masters patrolling the boundaries."

Mike nodded. "Maasdahs p'tol."

"Then there are other runaway slaves to worry about."

"Ronway Lezzahs," he said.

"Not to mention the people hanging out in the woods."

"Ronways too," Mike explained.

"And we'd still have to worry about slave-takers."

A nervous look came over Mike's face. "Tay-kuhs. Bad. Bad f'you. Breeduh."

Peg caught that right away, even without the mental subtext. *Bad for you. You're a Breeder.*

She fixed him with a long look. "Y'know, Mike, either you're picking up a lot of English from me, or I'm making sense of a lot of your language awful quick."

Mike just shrugged in response.

"If anybody picked me up here, I'd still be a Breeder, wouldn't I?"

"Nuh-uh," Mike said, with a grim look. Over his dead body.

Peg grinned at the effectiveness of the attitude adjustment she'd administered, then looked up to the sun, trying to gauge how many hours of light remained. "We'll need supplies if we're going into the woods." She flashed him a mental picture of the two of them creeping by cover of night into the forest, carrying bags. "What do we take?"

Mike patted his stomach—food, of course. Then he began beating his hands on his shoulders—warm clothes.

Peg looked north, where she could still feel the presence of Harry and, farther along, John. Then she nodded. "We'll make a list, and start collecting."

CHAPTER 14

"Graylaw Horry." Al, the forest chief, had a dubious expression on his face. Doubt filled his voice as well. "Wajawana geddownair?"

Harry Sturdley immediately translated: "Great Lord Harry, why would you want to go down there?"

"Goddafrenanair," Harry responded to the unhappy leader, "lessnadayway."

Despite his carrying heavy clout as the forest people's first official magic man, the tribe absolutely refused to join him in a trek southward. Thanks to their newfound communication, they'd been able to give him a long list of their fears—rival tribes, bandits, and slave-takers from the domain of the Masters. And while they appreciated his magic powers, they made it clear that their best defense was to avoid the area.

The best he'd gotten had been mental maps from some of the forest people that showed him where the Masters' settlement was located—a large cleared area to the south. That's where he'd find Peg, he was sure.

And Harry *had* to get there. Besides the constant reminder of Peg's location, he was getting recurrent intimations that she was in trouble.

So, with a woven bag of smoked elk meat over his shoulder and a rather tatty fur cape on his back,

Sturdley prepared to set off. Al cast a worried eye over him and tried a final attempt at dissuading him. "Bad place you're going to, Great Lord Harry. You're strong, but the Masters are big, and there's lots of them there. It's not like some little woods holding, with only one. They got a Master of Masters, and all."

"Don't you worry about me," Harry told Al. "Just be here where I can find you for the next three days."

"You remember the landmarks?" Al asked anxiously for about the tenth time.

"All here." Harry tapped his forehead. He had a detailed mental picture of the route he'd have to take.

With a wave to the members of the tribe, Harry set off along the game trail he'd been chased down not so long ago. That, Harry reminded himself, was before he'd discovered he had superpowers. He shrugged the weight of his fur cape to a more comfortable angle and walked onward. Except for the cape, he wasn't exactly dressed like a hero, in the stained ruins of his pearl gray slacks and a silk shirt. At least the tribeswomen had managed to disentangle all the blasted stickleberry branches that had been decorating him.

Maintaining a steady walking pace, Harry followed the trail ever southward. Every half hour or so, he'd stop to probe outward with his mind. So far, nobody was lying in ambush.

Harry continued with high confidence. It wasn't as though he'd never dealt with giants before. I negotiated quite a satisfactory deal with Robert back on Earth, didn't I? he reminded himself. And that was before I could read minds.

A great deal, a jeering voice muttered deep inside—a deal that got you set up to be murdered with John.

Harry repressed his doubts, thinking instead of Peg Faber. Hang on, Peg, he said. Sturdley's on his way. It reminded him of that weird dream he'd had in the INS detention center, the one where he'd been a superhero.

I really am one now—sort of, he thought. I have the power to control men's minds.

Even the sour voice in the back of his skull had to agree—as long as he didn't get netted, smashed on the head, or shot from afar.

"Damn," Harry muttered. "I knew there was something else I wanted to ask Al and the tribe. I wonder if anybody around here has invented bows and arrows yet?"

John Cameron awoke to a blinding light glaring in his face. He blinked blearily, trying to pull himself together. Must be another quiet day at the Fantasy Factory. He'd dozed off and slumped back so his face was aimed right at the ceiling fluorescents . . .

Memories began to flow. Wait a second. He hadn't been at the office. He'd been in San Diego, at the convention.

For a second, he relived the horrible moment as the men in black drew their weapons; Loony Lonnie's doomed attack. Once again, John leapt to his feet, grabbing Harry Sturdley with one hand while he reached out to Peg with the other. She seemed to move toward him in slow motion. Then came the sudden sear of agony in his shoulder, and the vertiginous drop into the Rift.

Another scene—Peg kneeling over him, her face serious and pale, trying to be gentle, but it felt like she was pouring acid over his shoulder. Then into the Rift again, losing both her and Harry . . .

Now John's blinking eyes opened wide. Where was he? Where was Peg? His shoulder—

He tried to turn his head, but he might just as well have attempted to move a mountain. Then, all of a sudden, the mountain was falling on him, and John tumbled back into darkness.

Peg felt slightly more human as she sloshed in somewhat chilly wash water. While searching for supplies, they'd come upon a deserted laundry shack.

Whatever had happened to the people here had come on them suddenly. All the wash hadn't even been hung up on the clotheslines, and there were signs that the fires for heating the wash water had burnt out. But Peg hadn't been able to resist the temptation of the big, barrellike washtubs. Here was a chance to get a bath, and perhaps rid herself of the secondhand wildlife in her borrowed clothing.

Leaving Mike to stand guard, Peg had tried a new application of her mental powers on the fleas or whatever that were eating her alive. This time, her "bugs, begone!" spell had worked. Then she'd gratefully slipped into the chilly water of a soaking tub.

With a deep breath, she ducked her head beneath the surface, trying to wash out the accumulation of dirt, sweat, and twigs that had tangled among her curls in the course of her first day in the land of the giants.

She came back up, running her fingers through the tangles. The land of the giants—that's what this place was. Even her halting communication with Mike had shown this was no garden spot. On a good day, it seemed, Master society fell somewhere between feudalism and street-gang subculture.

Masters kept Lessers in line with their superior

strength and virtual invulnerability. Plus, Mike had explained, the Masters had the ability to read minds. Rebellion was a flat impossibility, and even escape was damned difficult.

Given such advantages, it was easy enough for a giant to round up a retinue of humans to take care of the mundanities of existence—like the care and feeding of the Master.

Mike himself had been a metalworker. Peg had been tempted to call him a blacksmith, but the mental pictures he'd shown her of his work hadn't involved iron. He'd forged bronze and copper, making kettles and sickle blades, and worked gold and silver into jewelry for his Master.

Given his previous life here in Master Heaven, Peg could understand the sandy-haired giant Thomas' bad attitude in New York. It must have taken a serious incentive to make him give up his regiment of slaves.

But there *had* been good reason, as Peg discovered—a power struggle. Might makes right wasn't just the hallmark of relations between Masters and Lessers. It also defined the pecking order of the giants.

The bizarre fistfight/mob violence she'd witnessed from behind the lean-to had been a normalization of relations between two Masters. They and their retinues had mixed it up, with the winner gaining dominance over the other giant and his Lessers. His new subordinate giant in tow, the victor had gone off to find another potential victim.

He'd have the advantage confronting a single Master, because he could send his liegeman to challenge first. Even if the challenged party won that fight, the fair-haired Master could then take on an exhausted opponent. In this way an ambitious Master might recruit himself a faction of other giants, intriguing for the highest office—Master of Masters—with a domain as large as a small state.

Until recently, this area had been such a domain. Peg had been impressed by Mike's mental picture of the former Master of Masters, a big, well-built man, the only giant Peg had ever seen with a beard. His dark hair had also been streaked with gray.

There were rigid taboos involved in Masterly politics. The basic rule was "not in front of the servants." Although Masters were expected to vie among themselves, even to fight each other publicly, these fights could not be to the death.

That explained the almost stately progress of the brawl between the two Masters. The winner had to obtain a knockdown without seriously harming his opponent. If the fair-haired guy who'd won the fracas had inadvertently killed the man he was fighting, his own life would have been forfeit.

However, rising to the rank of Master of Masters required the assassination of the present officeholder. The murder of the former lord of this domain had been well planned, but had unraveled when a foraging party of Lessers had unexpectedly appeared on the scene.

Mike had been one of the Lessers to come upon the killing. Through his eyes, she'd seen the still and bloody form of the former Master of Masters. She'd also seen the murderer—blond, perfect, and pale-faced when he realized he'd been discovered. His face was as familiar to Peg as it was to Mike. The assassin of the old leader had been Robert.

The foragers had split up and run for their lives. Under the rules of the game, if Robert succeeded in catching and silencing them all before word got out, his gamble would still succeed. But Mike and a few others had eluded Robert's pursuit, and the giant had been rendered anathema for his transgression of the law—or rather, for getting caught at it. He'd been cast out of the domain, every Master's hand raised against him.

The domain itself had dissolved in civil war as various ambitious factions tried to beat their way to the top. Those giants who had followed Robert—Thomas was one—had suffered severely. Then they'd disappeared, secretly murdered, according to local Lesser gossip.

Mike wasn't so sure of that theory. One of those who'd disappeared was the daughter of the late Master of Masters, a political prize as well as a beauty. Peg was less than surprised to find she could identify the image in Mike's mind yet again.

The girl was Barbara.

She'd detected an image of the giantess before, in Mike's gallery of ideal women. At the time, she'd been impressed at the wealth of physical detail he'd been able to put into her picture. Now Peg found the source of Mike's knowledge—on earlier foraging expeditions, he'd stumbled across Robert and Barbara making love. From his images, it had been a pretty volcanic coupling.

Peg ducked her head underwater again. The machinations in this place were worse than daytime TV. The ambitious young stud screwing the boss' daughter. Peg suddenly felt a chill that had nothing to do with water temperature. Barbara had to know that Robert had killed her father. No way would she have willingly gone with him to Earth—

Unless she were in on the murder plot.

Peg stood in the tub, gasping a little. And these are the people Harry thinks of as *heroes*. John was right to distrust them.

She climbed out of the tub and checked to see how her underthings were drying.

Damn, I should have thought of a towel before I went in.

Peg pulled a shapeless shift over her damp hair and stepped outside. Mike turned, smiling, then looked a little shocked.

Why? Peg wondered—because I'm dressed like a girl?

She looked down and found the damp cloth was a bit too revealing. Mike's eyes immediately went to the horizon.

Wonderful, Peg thought, I've created a prude.

She walked over to the clothesline, checking the wash the vanished launderers had hung up to dry—several days ago if Peg were any judge. She was in luck, finding a suit of softer homespun that was only a bit too large. Retreating to the shack, she put the garment on.

Okay, I'm clean and bugless, Peg told herself. What's next?

She raided the line for extra clothing for herself and Mike. It wasn't easy finding something to fit his blacksmith's shoulders, but she managed to find a jacket that wasn't too small for him, and a jerkin-type garment that wasn't too large on her. She bundled her finds inside one of the voluminous garments and swung it over her shoulder.

"Now for some food," she told him, rubbing a hand on her stomach.

* * *

The shadows were growing longer as Peg and Mike at last headed for the boundary of the giant's domain. Besides the bundle of clothing, they now had a sack filled with ham and bread, some dried peas, grain, and a couple of gourd canteens. It represented all they could save from a burnt-out slave barracks. Mike had rescued the ham from its hiding place high in the eaves of the roof.

They were as ready as they'd ever be for their escape. Now they only had to wait for darkness. Mike led the way, taking a circuitous route. Instead of walking exposed through the hay stubble, they crept through one of the unharvested grainfields.

It would be a tough winter for the Lessers, Peg thought, unless a Master of Masters imposed some sort of order mighty fast.

She couldn't shake a feeling of oppression as they skulked through the head-high grain, and kept using her newfound mental powers to probe for anyone lurking.

So far, she hadn't caught any watchers in the rye.

The end of the field came with surprising suddenness. One second there seemed to be an infinity of grain stalks ahead of them. Then Mike was putting out a hand to halt her, the stalks thinned, and Peg could see open ground ahead.

Apparently it was the Masters' practice to harvest the fields closest to the woods first. Peg supposed that system made sense in a prison-type culture, depriving would-be escapees of any cover on their dash for the trees.

Even as they looked, Peg saw the second hurdle to be overcome—guards.

A twenty-foot-tall figure strolled along the edge of

the forest, accompanied by a couple of dozen jogging humans. The Master seemed to prefer the shade of the leafy canopy to the dwindling sunlight. He sat himself down with his back to a tree trunk, waving for his escort to stop.

After a few minutes, another patrol appeared, led by another Master. These two must have been faction-brothers, Peg realized, since they didn't confront each other with hostility. Instead, the Masters greeted each other in a friendly manner as their Lessers hunkered down.

The two giants talked for a few minutes, then one turned to a servant. Immediately, the human reached into a sack and produced a wrapped bundle. His Master untied it and produced the contents, which he shuffled.

Peg couldn't believe it. The giant had a pack of cards. The other Master cut the deck, there was another shuffle, then the first giant dealt two hands. Both giants considered their cards, then turned to their servants. Fingers pointed, and human servants rose to stand between the Masters. The card players considered each other, then more servants were called over.

The giant who'd dealt laid out his cards. His opponent shook his head in disgust, followed by a disdainful wave of his hand. All the servants who'd stood between the two of them went to sit beside the dealer.

"I don't believe this," Peg breathed. "They play cards—with people as chips?"

She turned to Mike, who only nodded. From out of his memory came images of major card games of the past. Sometimes hundreds of Lessers had changed hands on a single turn of the cards.

"What happens if a Master loses all of his people?" Peg asked.

Mike showed her another memory. It was a torch-lit scene, a card game that had obviously been going on for hours. One of the gigantic players had only a handful of humans around him. His back was stiff as he played on desperately.

Inevitably, he lost everything.

Players and giant kibitzers mocked the loser, who staggered to his feet and turned from the firelight. It was another familiar face, Maurice.

The busted giant turned back, his hands out to the players. One of the kibitzers leapt up and struck Maurice full in the face. He stumbled back, and the other giant kept swinging, running after him, jeering.

Peg shook her head. "Another rule?"

Mike nodded. "Lose all Lessers," he said in that half-understandable argot, "not Master anymore. Fair game. Can beat, even kill, unless he goes into woods and finds new Lessers to serve him."

"Charming," Peg muttered, settling in to watch the game go on. There was no other entertainment available, and they still had hours to kill until true darkness.

As she found herself a comfortable pose, Peg reviewed the facts she'd learned about the giant immigrants now on her world. One was an assassin, one a deposed slave-owner, one a patricidal bitch, and one an inept loser, she thought. When it came to creating superheroes, Harry could really pick 'em.

It was after moonset, deep into the night, but Rosalind was still awake. Hunger increased her restlessness, and this was her third day without a decent meal. She had found some berries and drunk from a stream, but that hardly took the edge off a ravenous appetite. Most of the berries had smeared on her foot-long fingers as she tried to separate them from the bushes, and the small amount she'd garnered were not enough to satisfy a twenty-foot frame.

Rosalind lay beneath a tree, staring up into the dark beyond its branches, hands across her empty stomach. She'd never realized how difficult it was to forage for oneself. There had always been Lessers to handle those demeaning tasks. But the last of her servants had disappeared into the forest yesterday, as they fled a patrol from the domain. Maybe her people had been taken by woods-runners, or perhaps they served to swell the retinue of that miserable Calvin who had tried to pursue her.

At least she'd escaped. The domain was no longer a safe place for females of her race—not with all the barriers down. She'd heard stories from the time before the last Master of Masters had restored order, of women treated no better than the Lessers' breeding-women . . .

But hunger might well drive her back to the clearings. Without a retinue, she couldn't eat. Single-handed, she couldn't hunt up enough food. And although she had searched hard this last day, she had found no woods-runners to impress into her service. How did others manage it? she wondered.

A hollow sound rumbled from her stomach. Gods below, Rosalind swore, if this kept up she'd *have* to return to the domain and submit to whoever would have her, just to stay alive. If only there were *some* Lessers to serve her!

A thread of detection tickled the outer borders of her immaterial senses. Thoughts.

Sending out the briefest probe of her immaterial powers, she breathed a sigh of relief. No, it wasn't a Master. These were Lessers—a pair of runaways, it felt like.

The answer to her prayer.

She could capture them, bind them tightly to her mind, erase their wills completely, make them serve her mindlessly. It was frowned on by her society, considered *déclassé*. But right now, it was necessary.

Rosalind stepped into the path of the runaways.

The Lesser female looked up and froze.

"Mike," she said to her companion, "we've got big trouble."

CHAPTER 15

John Cameron swam back to awareness. He still didn't know where he was, but he remembered his experience with the glaring light the last time he'd come to. Now he slit his eyes, trying to see past the light—but without any success.

He felt weak, but not as hopelessly fogged as he'd been in his previous brush with consciousness. Lying quietly, he tried to take physical stock. The pain in his shoulder was gone, although he was aware, somehow, of damage to the tissues there. In fact, he suddenly realized, not only was there no pain, there seemed to be no sensation at all from his body. He felt as through her were floating in midair.

John laboriously turned his head, forcing back a wave of nausea that surged at his slightest movement. Okay. A clean bandage covered the shoulder wound. And apparently he'd been given a potent anesthetic.

He'd have to thank Peg for keeping enough blood inside him until they reached wherever this place was to patch him up.

Peg. The memory of those final, nightmarish moments in the Rift came back to him once again. He'd all but blacked out, lost control of the transition. His last conscious memory had been horror as first Peg, then Harry slipped way.

Had he gotten them through? If so, where were they? Flung out at random somewhere on the face of this world . . . or were they still lost in the Rift?

He had to try and find them—save them! He forced himself to sit upright, his body moving like a machine with rusty controls.

For a brief instant, John saw that he was in the center of a large, dark room—a room that seemed to spiral wildly around him.

Then he collapsed and, once again, darkness descended.

Rosalind loomed over the two runaways. For what she intended to do, it was best to begin from a dominating position. The act of Binding had all sorts of ritual accretions that made the practice rare today. Then, too, most Masters made use more of their physical rather than mental powers.

Rosalind was an exception—and her immaterial powers were strong. She could discern the fright rising from the pair below her. That would be her opening. She sent probes through the fear, tracing it to its source in the Lessers' brains, enhancing it to hold them immobile.

The first step of Binding was done.

Peg Faber's heart hammered under her ribs like a wild thing trying to escape a cage. She'd often heard the expression "feet rooted by fear." Now she was living it.

The figure poised over her was female, with long black hair and a beautiful, if cold and calculating, face.

But Peg found herself reliving those terrifying moments when Thomas had advanced on her and John, the promise of death in the sandy-haired giant's eyes.

Beside her, Mike had dropped to his knees, moaning in terror.

Wait a second, Peg thought. He's dealt with Masters before. Mike's memory of finding Robert over the dead body of the Master of Masters came to her. He hadn't broken down like this back then. No, he'd run like hell, as fast as his feet could move.

Something is wrong, here, she realized. Something is *definitely* wrong.

A new wave of terror flooded through Peg, wiping away all clarity, all rational thought. Mike was on the ground now, his eyes shut tight, tears dribbling from under the lids. But Peg dug in her mental heels. This isn't like me at all, she thought. Even when those guys were going to rape me, I didn't freeze up this way.

Her eyes went up to the giantess staring down at them. This has to be coming from outside my mind—from *her*! Now that she had something to fight against, Peg pushed against the panic, and it receded.

Then it was coming back, stronger than before.

But Peg wasn't filled with fear. Anger also suffused her being. *Goddamit, get out of my head!* she raged.

Sheer fury battered away the fright like a high wind shredding fog. Peg glared upward, panting as if she'd run an endurance race. The face of the female Master was a picture of shock. An unguarded tendril of thought floated past Peg's supersensitized mind.

The Breeder resists!

Damn right! Peg thought.

The face above her tightened, and Peg reeled from a new attack. Instinctively, she fought to raise barriers against the probes of thought. The attacks were blunted, then stopped.

A trace of fear crept into the giantess' expression. Then the attack was redoubled.

This time the probes didn't try to smash through Peg's mental defenses. Like the insidious tendrils of some killer plant, they slid across Peg's shields, trying to edge around them.

Peg visualized a globe around her herself, a nimbus of energy to repel the invading thought-probes. To Peg's mind, they scratched at her construct, then the tendrils seemed to cover it like ivy. Her globe of protection was surrounded, then *squeezed.*

The pressure drove in on Peg's mental shields.

They were overextended, she realized, trying to defend too much space around her.

Peg managed to shrink her defensive perimeter, bolstering it, and for a moment, the situation stabilized. But the pressure built up again.

Inexorably, Peg's shields shrunk again and again, until they finally couldn't protect her entire body.

The giantess lashed out with a new blast of lethal energy, aimed not at Peg's mind, but her corporeal self.

For Peg, it was like having a leg struck by lightning. Nerves were activated, axons triggered, and suddenly agony invaded her brain. Peg dropped as if someone had cut her off at the knees. Worse, she was aware of the giantess' mental probes twirling around the sensations invading her mind.

Anger flared again. As she had blasted back the fear, Peg now blasted back the pain, channeling its return along the connection the female Master had built.

Peg had a moment's triumph as the darkly handsome

face above her showed pain. The giantess actually stumbled back, her bare breasts heaving.

Fury replaced shock, and hammer-blows of psychic energy smashed against Peg's defenses. She was down on hands and knees, her ears ringing, grimly trying to spin out a shield, to keep from being crushed out of consciousness.

Mike stirred beside her. Apparently, the giantess was devoting so much of herself to Peg, she'd forgotten the other runaway.

The heavily muscled young man pushed himself upright, his wide eyes going from Peg to the giantess. Peg had no idea what he saw, but somehow he perceived the struggle in progress.

And he loved Peg.

Mike stumbled to the margin of the forest path, where a dead tree spread sere branches to the sky. He leapt, wrenching off a lower limb, and advanced on the female Master waving his makeshift weapon.

With a wild cry, Mike charged. The giantess stared down, her eyes going wider in shock. This was not at all the way she'd expected this encounter to go.

The huge face above them tightened in a new determination. Peg didn't need psychic powers to read the message in those big, dark eyes. The giantess had decided to kill them.

Moving with deliberation, the woman raised her right foot to stomp down on the charging Lesser.

The physical action caused a weakening in the attack on Peg, but crouched on the ground as she was, that fact barely impinged on her consciousness. Peg saw what the giantess planned to do through half-closed eyes, and something seemed to snap inside the castaway's brain.

"Dammit, *NO*!" she shrieked, lashing out with every emotion roaring through her being.

Perhaps it was the unexpected surge of strength from a seemingly defeated enemy, or the distraction of allocating resources between mental and physical attacks. Peg's mind-bolt hit a juncture in the female Master's shields. It tore through, and suddenly Peg was in the giantess' mind.

She caught a bit of ego-identification: the name Rosalind.

Well, good night, Rosalind.

She'd learned from her tinkering with Mike's mind—from her mental blast that had almost killed him.

Peg thrust probes into Rosalind's memories, into her lower brainstem. She wiped out conscious memory of this encounter while turning off higher mental functions.

Above her, Rosalind lurched, her eyes going blank. Then the giantess toppled over into a tree.

Mike stumbled to a stop, his arms lowering his hopeless club. He took in the spectacle of the defeated Master with the slack-faced look of someone watching his entire world turned upside-down. Then he twisted round to Peg, his eyes wide.

She made a beckoning gesture. "Come on, we've got to get out of here."

When Mike came close enough, she just about dropped against his shoulder. "And I'll need a little help for the first few miles."

Peg shut her eyes. She felt as if her head had been used as a clapper for one of the bells at Notre Dame. The path seemed distorted as she stumbled along with Mike's aid, the ground swelling and dipping beneath her suddenly clumsy steps. The focus of Peg's personality, the spot where she felt she was, seemed somehow divorced from her body, as if her soul were floating ten feet ahead or four feet behind her physical presence. She'd felt that way before, after some intense drunken bashes back in college. But she was cold sober now.

Then they heard an uproar behind them. When Peg glanced back, she "saw" far beyond the first curve of their twisting course. A male giant stood over Rosalind's supine form, his eyes gleaming in the reflected torchlight of dozens of servitors.

The flickering illumination danced on both giant bodies as the Master knelt beside the unconscious female, reaching out a hand—

Peg's throat tightened as she detected lust even at this distance.

There was one good thing. The milling crowd of voyeuristic servitors had obliterated their physical trail.

The hammering pain in Peg's head lessened as she and Mike continued on, sinking to a dull throb with each step she took. That odd dissociation faded as well, as her mind came to dwell inside her body once more. Soon she was able to walk on her own.

Centered again, Peg forced herself to throw out occasional psychic probes. It was like exercising a muscle she'd already overstrained, but the experience with the giantess had convinced Peg of the necessity for the earliest possible warning.

Casting back along their trail, Peg stiffened as her filament of thought brushed another consciousness. Delicately, she firmed up the connection until she got a glimpse from one of the followers' eyes.

Three men, clothed in furs, carrying spears. One of

them knelt, studying the ground intently. Checking their tracks, Peg realized.

"Mike," she whispered, "more trouble. We have to speed up."

They increased their pace, but soon Peg was holding onto the big man's arm again. The fight with the giantess had stolen what remained of her strength.

She brought them to a halt, panting and dizzy, wobbling in Mike's arms.

He'll have to carry me, she thought. And if those guys catch up with us while Mike's got his arms full, we won't even be able to put up a fight.

Huddled against Mike's broad chest, Peg launched another probe along the trail behind them. She blinked. Had she missed their pursuers?

Peg probed back farther along the trail, and stiffened as she detected more minds.

Oh, God, she thought, what if the first bunch were only the advance guard?

Peg narrowed in again and realized she had overshot. This was a slaving party from the detachment led by the horny giant. If they hadn't found Peg and Mike's footprints, the slavers must be on the trail of the three hairy guys.

She pulled her exhausted body into Mike's arms. "Run," she whispered.

Mike took Peg at her word, settling her comfortably and heading off at a good clip. Moments later, they heard cries of consternation behind them. Their trackers had found the running footprints.

Peg shuddered. They were damned close—closer than she thought.

The only hope was that the pursuers yet farther back

would hear the noise and speed up their pursuit as well.

Mike jolted along, trying to do a good impersonation of Mr. Rush. Unfortunately, he wasn't the superspeedy Fantasy Factory hero. He was only a human, a big, muscular one, but one who had also been in fights—both physical and mental—that day. Mike's gasping lungs had his chest working like a bellows.

"Just a little farther—around this next bend," Peg told him. "Then I'll get down and we'll get off this damned path."

But when Mike rounded the bend, he didn't stop to set Peg down. Instead, he tossed her into an open space between two bushes and kept running. "I'll go on," he flung over his shoulder, "leave a trail for them to follow, then turn off. You'll find me without tracks."

Peg had no time to argue with him before he dashed off. She headed deeper into the forest, groping her way between tree trunks, flashing a nervous probes both along their backtrail and up the path to Mike. His mind seemed like a distant, faint spark.

An alien sound penetrated the trees—the thud of approaching footfalls on the path. Their pursuers were quite near. Peg wriggled her way through a thicket of berry bushes, trying to zero in on Mike. How far away had he gotten?

More footfalls signaled that at last the cavalry had arrived—or rather, the infantry from the Masters' domain. The would-be hairy bushwhackers were totally surprised by the Master's slavers, but judging from the noise level the fight was still sharp.

Peg plunged on through complete darkness. This was their last chance. They had to develop an unbeatable lead during the fight, or the slave-takers would be after them, too. She stumbled down a gully and floundered through a small stream, once again soaking the old pair of Keds she'd pulled on an unknown time ago in another world.

Casting out again with her immaterial senses, Peg located Mike. Good. She was still moving on an intercept course.

Peg kept her head down, making the best time she could through the rough country. She soon realized that the respite of being carried had *not* recharged her batteries. She was plodding rather than walking.

A quick scan back to the path brought her a sigh of relief. The slave-takers had apparently decided to keep the three hairy Lessers in hand rather than searching for two more in the bush.

A sweep ahead showed Mike not too far away. Bolstered by optimism, Peg managed to put a little more speed into her step.

Judging that the slave-takers were safely out of earshot, she risked a low call. "Mike?"

She heard a soft whistle ahead and to her left. Still scanning for possible pursuit, she aimed herself in the direction of the quiet signal.

A wall of bushes blocked her way, and when she pushed through them, Peg stopped in surprise, her face staring up at starlight. A rocky outcrop poked from the earth, barren except for a few tufts of grass. Mike had chosen a sheltered spot in the lee of some large rocks and was busily homemaking—in this case piling dry leaves into the hollow for mattresses. He'd already dragged over some brush for concealment.

When Peg made her weary way out of the forest, Mike's face lit up. He dropped his load and rushed over to her, scooping her up in his arms again.

You'd think I was fine china, the way he's carrying me, Peg groused to herself.

But her head slowly came down to rest on his broad shoulder.

Well, she thought muzzily, I guess here's where I find out if I've really taught him to be a gentleman. Mike brought her to the hollow and gently put her down on a hummock of leaves. Peg lay back with a grateful sigh. Smiling, Mike went to one knee beside her.

Then a human figure came round from behind the boulders.

Mike's soft expression transformed into a frantic snarl. He flung himself across the little hollow, going into a roll.

When he came up on his feet, the tree-branch club he'd broken off in the forest was in his right hand.

Eyes glued to the amorphous figure still in the shadow of the boulder, Mike circled round, trying to see if there were more visitors. Not detecting anybody else, he came smoothly forward, club raised to brain the intruder.

"Mike! Hold it!" Peg cried.

She had finally pulled together enough energy to send a mental probe.

The caped figure stepped into the dim glimmer of the stars. "Glad to see you, Red."

It was Harry Sturdley.

CHAPTER 16

"H-Harry?" Peg breathed, her face pale as she finally wrestled Mike's club down from attack position.

"In the flesh—and the bearskin," Sturdley said with a laugh. His words were cut off as Peg dashed past her companion and flung her arms around Harry in a wild hug.

"I . . . I was afraid." Peg's voice was tight with tears, and she rested her forehead against Harry's chest.

"I wouldn't do that, Red," Harry said, gently disentangling himself. "This cape has a lot of co-tenants." He hunched his lean shoulders under the heavy fur and began to scratch.

Choking back a combined sob and laugh, Peg reached out with her mind and ordered, "Bugs, begone!"

Sturdley's eyebrows rose. "So all that mental heavy hitting I was detecting from miles away *was* you! You've wound up with superpowers, just like me."

Peg shook her head. "I wouldn't exactly call them superpowers."

"Hey, at the very least, you can command bugs. We may have a new heroine when we get back home—Bug Girl! She can face off against the Roach—helpful insects versus the vermin he commands. It'll be—"

"Don't you mean, *if* we get home?" Peg asked, pain in her eyes.

Harry's eyes went unfocused for a second. "I can still detect John."

She did the same. "But he hasn't moved."

"After taking a slug, I wouldn't *expect* him to move," Sturdley told her. "He's lying low and recovering."

"Or maybe the unmoving John we're detecting is only his d-dead body," Peg choked.

Mike didn't understand the rapid exchange in English, but he could see that the stranger was upsetting Peg. He stepped forward grimly, his club at the ready.

"So who's your friend, Red?" Sturdley asked.

Peg quickly told the story. Harry's eyebrows lifted higher. "Hoo. I knew it was a woman's prerogative to change *her* mind, but other people's, too? You *did* get powers."

"Well, I think I sprained my brain," Peg said, rubbing temples that seemed to ache in time with her heartbeat. "I am completely wiped out."

"Then maybe it's time for some shut-eye." Harry glanced into the little bower Mike had arranged. "Any room in there for another boarder?"

Harry suddenly turned to the forest, alerted by some movement there. "Perhaps it's better if we sleep in shifts. I think a guard would be a good idea."

He offered to take the first watch, and with Peg translating, Mike agreed to take the second. With their security all arranged, Peg crawled off to her mattress of leaves and knew no more.

She awoke the next morning somewhat stiff from roughing it, and realized she'd slept through the night.

"I was supposed to take the last shift!" Peg complained. "Why didn't you wake me up?"

"I took a little more time, and so did muscle-boy here," Harry responded. He gave her a long, searching glance. "Last night, your face looked like a sheet with two holes poked in it. Even now you've got bags under your bags."

Peg grimaced. "Thanks, Harry. You really know how to make a girl feel good about herself."

Mike led them in foraging for breakfast. They made do on a few handfuls of nuts and berries with slices of ham from their supply sack, then set off with Harry in the lead.

"I don't know what you two intended to do out here in the forest," he said, glancing at Peg and her muscular companion. "But I've hooked up with a tribe of people living out here."

"Mike told me that the woods-runners can be pretty savage," Peg said.

"He's right," Sturdley said grimly. "At our first meeting, they wanted to use me for target practice—sort of like the staff meetings back home." He grinned. "Luckily, I was able to use my new mental powers to give them a big magic act. Now I'm the tribe's Wise Old Man—the Graylaw Horry."

With Sturdley acting as guide and Mike as scoutmaster, they moved easily through the forest toward Harry's rendezvous. Peg and Harry spelled each other on mentally scanning the area, easing the strain on their powers and further refining their use.

Twice they detected the presence of potential enemies, and the group stopped to hide. The first alarm turned out to be a miserable-looking extended family of forest people, wandering a little too close to the

Masters' domain. The other was more serious, a carefully set up ambush at the junction of two trails. Harry had detected the presence of dozens of Lesser slave-takers lurking in the brush, and Peg pinpointed a Master kneeling in the shadow of one of the trees.

The travelers immediately left the path, setting off through the forest to give the slave-takers as wide a berth as possible.

Thanks to the detour, it was late afternoon before Harry finally recognized the landmarks he'd burned into his memory. "We're pretty close now," he announced.

Mike threw back his head, inhaling deeply. "Smoke," he announced in his dialect. "Cooking fire."

Following Harry's directions and Mike's nose, they soon reached the camp of the little tribelet.

"We'd better make some noise," Harry said to his fellow travelers. "Don't want Al and the folks to think we're sneaking up on them."

"Hey, Al," he called, shouting for the group's chieftain.

For a second, the murmur of camp noise in the distance ceased. Then Al and the three male members of the clan appeared, spears in hand.

"Graylaw Horry!" the leader of the hunter's band said with a big smile.

If someone invented dentistry here, they could make a fortune, Peg thought, seeing the chief's cracked, discolored teeth.

"Al, this is Peg," Harry said, pointing to his erstwhile assistant. "And this is Mike."

The men of the tribe seemed happy to greet a new female, but were dubious about Mike. Al went squinty-eyed at Mike's bulk and size. Why welcome a possible rival for his leadership position? Wilf and Rafe, the two men with wives and children, saw no need to take on a new member. Ken, the unmarried man, liked Mike least of all. He stood to lose the most status.

Ken, in fact, raised his spear for a cast. The other tribe members stood like statues of disapproval staring at the stranger.

Do something, Harry, Peg sent mentally to her boss. *I had to futz with this guy's mind. I can't just turn him loose because he won't be popular.*

Sturdley made a peremptory gesture toward Ken, and the young man lowered his spear.

"I bring help for your tribe," Harry said, falling into the local patois. "My friend the wise woman, and her friend, a good, strong man. Why do you want to stick them?"

"Not the beauty," Ken bust out. "But him!"

Mike obviously understood. He took up a protective stance beside Peg.

"Don't need more men," Ken said to the other tribesmen. "Got enough mouths to feed now."

Harry jerked a thumb at Mike. "He's a strong hunter and a brave warrior. We need him."

Al stepped forward, letting his spearpoint trail in the ground. He clapped a callused hand to Mike's biceps. "Strong," he agreed.

"We'll need him," Harry repeated. "He has many things to tell me. And he'll serve us both." He turned to Mike. "Right?"

Mike glanced at Peg, who nodded. Shrugging, Mike nodded, too.

Al relaxed. "Then we take him."

The married members of the tribe went along with their chief. Ken scowled, but was outvoted.

They traveled on to the camp, where the scene was repeated, this time with the women disapproving of Peg. Harry sighed. Probably it was natural. The tribeswomen's primitive existence had scoured most traces of beauty out of them. They looked on Peg as sexual competition, what with her face, figure, and in their eyes, fancy homespun clothes. Al and the married men pushed the issue through, however.

Janey, the chief's wife, took this development with ill grace, especially when she saw Al's appreciative glance as Peg removed her outer jerkin. The woman tried to establish her dominance by shoving Peg over to the cook-fire.

Peg, however, was not about to be turned into a kitchen slave. She whipped around, going into a martial-arts stance. Harry grimaced. Peg was the terror of the Fantasy Factory's more amorous artists, having disabled several drawing hands when they got too grabby. But was this the time for a karate demonstration?

Harry quickly intervened. "Janey, Peg won't be doing woman things. She's with me."

As an attempt to fix Peg's status, his action failed miserably. As scandal, however, it was wildly successful. All eyes in the camp went from Harry to Peg. Even without his powers, Harry could read the thoughts behind Janey's shocked expression. *The dirty devil! And at his age!*

Mike scowled, but Peg's eyes twinkled.

If I were twenty-five years younger, Red, you wouldn't find this situation so funny, Harry thought. Twenty years. Even ten.

Peg gave him a low chuckle. "You got us into this,

Harry," she muttered. "You get us out. In the meanwhile, I'm going to wash up."

The tribespeople turned elaborately away as she walked off.

Great, Harry thought. She's pushed from kitchen slave to the magic-man's sex toy. I suppose we'll have to give a sample of her powers before things calm down.

He sniffed appreciatively at the roasting meat.

After dinner.

Peg shivered as she knelt in the shallow stream, sluicing freezing water over her naked body. I'll probably end up giving myself pneumonia if I keep adhering to twentieth-century ideals of cleanliness around here, she told herself. Except for the giants, everyone she'd met on this world had been pretty ripe—even Mike. She'd have to get used to it, she decided, scrubbing under her arms. But not just yet.

She was rubbing some water into her face when she caught a flicker of movement in the brush.

Peg leapt to her feet, moving toward her clothes laid out on some rocks. The watcher in the bushes got there ahead of her, moving into the open.

It was Ken.

He leered as he ran his eyes down her body.

Peg stood with the water barely up to her knees, one arm across her bosom, her other hand shielding the apex of her thighs—the pose for a classic statue, "Woman Surprised."

This is what I get for thinking I was safe with Harry's friends, Peg thought. Memo for the future: Always scan before making yourself vulnerable.

Ken swaggered down to the bank of the stream until

he actually stood on her clothing. "Y'can put your hands down," he said in the local patois. "I've seen it all already." He grinned nastily, his hands on his hips. "Right tasty."

Then he started to undo his leather breeches. "A waste for all that to go just to an old man. I'll show you what a young 'un can do. You'll like it lots better."

"What I'd like best of all," Peg said stonily, "is for you to *go soak your head*!"

She reached out with immaterial powers, seizing control of muscles. Ken's legs began shuffling forward, his breeches still caught around his knees. He almost reached the stream bank when he finally tripped, falling heavily on the pebbled surface.

Ken tried to fling out his arms to break his fall, but they stayed stiff-braced at his side. The would-be Romeo lay gasping for breath, his face inches above the running water.

"Cool off," Peg told him. "I told you to go soak your head."

Ken's neck muscles relaxed, dropping his face into the rippling current. The shock of the cold water made Ken gasp, then choke as liquid invaded his windpipe. He tried to thrash, to pull his head back, but his own muscles kept his head under. His lungs began to burn, and little red lights appeared at the back of his eyes. Blackness threatened to swallow him.

Then, at the very last minute, his body was free. He arched away from the surface of the stream, coughing and choking, making horrible retching noises.

Weak as a kitten, he rolled over to find Peg standing over him, now fully dressed.

"That's just a taste of what I can do," she told him. "The next time *this*"—she nudged a very limp organ with the toe of her sneakers—"gives you trouble, take a long, cold bath."

The tribe was just gathering for dinner when Peg returned with a chastened, very bedraggled-looking Ken in tow. The young hunter was soaked from the chest up. He rushed over to the fallen log where Harry sat and dropped to his knees. In a trembling voice, he begged forgiveness, outlining his transgression and the results.

From the corner of his eye, Harry took in the very silent band around him.

So much for defining her status, he thought. Peg had come up with a real convincing demonstration all by herself.

Full darkness had fallen by the time they'd finished eating. Flickering firelight danced on Al's features as he turned to Harry. "Will you lead?" he asked.

Nonplussed, Harry kept a poker face and shook his head negatively. "You do it, Al."

The chief moved closer to the fire and began a ritual chant.

Once we ruled.
Fathers of our fathers' fathers, once they ruled.
Ruled the world.
But they sinned.
Punished then by gods below, for their sin.
World grew cold.
Masters came.
They enslaved us, ceaseless toiling . . .
Gods below!

There was a moment's silence, then Al began the chant again. The other tribe members picked it up. Mike joined in, too, though he kept looking nervously over his shoulder as if he expected a disapproving Master to appear. The tribespeople slapped their hands against logs or beat their feet on the earth to the rhythm of the chant. Then they all were silent.

Harry and Peg stared at each other from their places on a long log. Letting a few minutes go by, Harry beckoned the chief over. "Al, how long ago did the Masters come?"

The chief could only shrug. "Long and long ago," he said. "We don't know."

"And do you have any other chants or stories from the times before then?"

Again, Al could only shrug helplessly. "Our oldest stories are hunting stories. Maybe from the time of my grandfather's grandfather."

Harry sent him back closer to the fire. "They're preliterate," he said to Peg. "There's no history beyond current events and legends."

"Murky ones, at that," Peg said. "Too bad these people didn't have a Homer. Then perhaps we'd have an epic about the wrath of 'the gods below.' "

She shrugged. "The domains are illiterate, too. Mike has never seen writing, even among the Masters. Messages are sent by word of mouth. If the receiver wants the message to be a secret, he . . . erases . . . the messenger."

Sturdley shook his head. "Kills them, you mean."

"They live by almost neolithic farming. The only metalworking is for the giants' jewelry—and a couple of small, crude agricultural implements. The Lessers—that's what the humans are called—are treated like kennel dogs." Peg shuddered. "And the women are treated like bitches in heat."

She stared at Harry, trying to convey the horror.

"Humans are nothing to them. They use us as poker chips when they play cards. That's the world your heroes come from, Harry."

"The world they left," Harry put in. "A world they hated and couldn't change."

Peg's gray eyes went fierce and cold. "You keep fooling yourself, Harry. You made excuses. You wouldn't listen to John. Well, you're going to hear *me.*"

She told him what she had learned from Mike about Maurice and Robert, Thomas and Barbara. Peg explained what it meant to be a Master of Masters, and then related the murder of the last holder of that title—how Robert had committed it, and her suspicions about Barbara's connivance in the deed.

"They're a very nasty bunch from a nasty social system," she finished. "They created chaos here, then ran to our world when things started going against their faction."

Sturdley stared toward the fire with blind eyes. "No wonder John was so scared of them," he finally muttered. "They're monsters, and I gave them the key to New York City." He glanced at her. "You two were right. I should have listened."

He drew himself up on his log seat, his face tightening. "We've got to get back—and not just to shake the dust of this crazy planet off our shoes, either. Who knows what the giants are doing to the city—to our world—while we're stuck here?"

To a casual, distant observer, it would have looked like a typical lakefront beach party—bonfires, scant clothing, nighttime swims, couples disappearing into the woods. Closer observation would have revealed that the celebrants were twenty feet tall.

Robert burst out of the water with a booming laugh, scooped up Barbara, who gave a few girlish shrieks, and dashed for the tree line. They stopped their noise as soon as they were in the sheltering shadows, and Robert let Barbara down. They walked a little farther into the woods, until they met Thomas and Ruth.

"Leave us," Robert told the redheaded giantess. She pulled her costume top back down and disappeared into the darkness. For a second, Thomas looked piqued as his leader squeezed water out of his damp blond hair.

"How is Gideon?" Barbara asked quietly.

"The same," Thomas responded with a shrug. The rebel giant had not regained consciousness after the beating Robert had given him. Unwilling to lose one of his people, even a traitor whose breeding potential was low, Robert had been forced to make a difficult decision. A mental canvass of local medical personnel had turned up a doctor engaged in illegal activities. It had been easy enough for Robert to ferret out proof, and Dr. Cedric Thonnegger had become theirs to order.

Thonnegger had managed to stabilize Gideon's condition, but the giant remained comatose. In the end, they'd had to move him to a carefully prepared facility—a new home for Thonnegger on the lake, with a boathouse converted for invalid care. Gideon had been moved by water under cover of darkness.

Since then, Robert had interested himself in all the available marvels of modern human medical technology—the life-support system to keep Gideon alive, the mechanical extraction of sperm samples in case Gideon passed on. And lately . . .

"Thonnegger was quite reluctant to undertake the new line of research I suggested," Robert said. "He tried to plead ignorance of nuclear medicine. Wanted to know why I wanted him to do radiation tolerance tests on Gideon."

"Nuclear medicine?" Barbara said in bafflement. "Radiation?"

"I've been devoting some thought and research to our problems here—Lessers that are far too numerous, too well-armed." Robert leaned against a tree, his voice becoming almost philosophical. "It strikes me that one problem might solve the other. Their greatest weapons are controlled by relatively few people. A finger on the button, as the Lessers say . . ."

He pushed away from the tree. "But first, we need some knowledge of what these weapons can do to *us*."

Robert stepped over to take Barbara's hand. "I'll leave to you the task of persuading the doctor, Thomas. Perhaps tomorrow night. I believe that's when you and Ruth are supposed to be out here in the forest."

To confuse the watchers on the shore, Robert still detailed pairs of giants to hide in the woods, even though Gideon wasn't there to be guarded anymore.

"Afterwards, you may enjoy her."

Peg and Harry huddled near to the fire, their heads close. "The question is," she said, "how do we catch up with John?"

"We know he's someplace to the north. That's where we'll be heading," Sturdley replied. His introspection was past. Now it was time to act, to make plans.

Peg wondered which comic-book storyline he'd plunder for his strategy. She hoped it wouldn't be Mr. Pain.

"Al!" Harry called the chief over again. "Let's draw a picture of the lands you know."

Al had never heard of a map, and was quite fascinated with the idea. Centering the universe on the spot where they now were, he was able to give a fairly detailed view of the near locality. The scale was hard to judge, though. Al tended to measure distances in terms of how many days' march.

Then, too, once outside the usual range of the tribe's travels, geography became a featureless blur. All Al could tell them was that there was a Great Water to the east, and a Lesser Water to the west—a sea, perhaps, or maybe a large river. Another big geographical unit lay to the north. It was known as the White Wall.

"Glaciers?" Peg wondered aloud. Maybe that was why this world seemed so cold—even the ancient chant had mentioned it. What if this world were going through an Ice Age?

She dismissed the thought as Harry abruptly changed the line of questioning. He no longer wanted to know about the land, but the people. Were there other Masterly domains? Were they different from here?

Al was able to give much less information there. His people had heard of other domains. Wilf and Sue, one of the couples in the tribe, had run away from a domain to the northwest. Judging from their stories, life was about the same. Al and his people didn't want to check it out. They spent their time staying as far away from Masters as possible.

"Is there trade between the domains?" Sturdley pressed. "Any contact? Communication? Would every human who passes close to a domain be treated like a slave?"

Al was completely ignorant in this regard. The information came, surprisingly, from Mike.

The burly metalworker remembered a few times when entertainers—minstrels—had visited the domain. Apparently, Masters tolerated them for their entertainment value. Even being all-powerful could be boring, it seemed. The minstrels had moved on to other pastures after a few performances through the domain.

Harry smiled wryly. "No matter where, it seems the old gypsy spirit pops up."

He frowned in thought, staring into the embers of the fire. "Okay," he said abruptly, slapping his hand against the fallen tree trunk. "Auditions are now open."

Peg blinked. "Auditions? For what?"

Harry gave her the sort of smile he usually saved for the media when announcing a new coup. "We're auditioning for the Graylaw Horry's Traveling Show. Better get that pretty ass in gear. The tour starts tomorrow."

CHAPTER 17

After a couple of weeks on the road, Graylaw Horry's Traveling Show had tightened up its act—as well as some of the performers, Harry thought. As they headed steadily north, the fifteen-mile marches per day had tautened Peg Faber's curves far more than weekly visits to her health club and dojo. The cheekbones were also more visible on her heart-shaped face, and stubborn freckles had cropped up on all her exposed skin.

With Harry and Peg both contributing to the larder by periodically luring some large game to the hunters' spears, the tribesfolk had lost their half-starved aspect. But the exercise of all-day walking left Harry Sturdley's naturally lean frame looking like a combination of leather and whipcord.

Both of the Earthpeople had retired their alien clothes and shoes, wearing moccasins for the daily hikes. Under Harry's design and Peg's guidance, they'd worked up costumes for performance as well as for wearing on the route of march. Mike had also contributed his skills in building a couple of hand-pulled carts for carrying the show's necessities.

Al and his people still looked a little dazed. They had moved ahead several centuries in living standards in the space of weeks. Suddenly they had more possessions than could fit in a series of skin satchels and wicker baskets. By the standards of this world, they'd become quite rich.

That was now a concern for Harry and Peg, forcing them to scan often through the now predominantly piney forests, searching for bandits or woods-runner tribes. The vehicles kept them tied to the trails, and several times they'd had to backtrack and take other routes to avoid hostile groups.

There had been more than enough of those, and ever-smaller pockets of what ran for civilization on this world. The domains had grown smaller along their travels, with less presence of the ruling class. Some hadn't even had Masters of Masters—they were just warring camps, where Harry's troupe had to give separate performances to avoid the risk of fights.

They had ventured hundreds of miles closer to wherever John Cameron might be found. Like the lodestar, the trace of his being drew them ever northward. The feeling of his presence was now very strong for Harry and Peg. But when they tried to drive probes toward that presence, they were unable to contact John's mind.

Harry responded to his doubts and misgivings in his usual way, burying them in work and more work. He'd ransacked Mike's memories of minstrel performances and planned a spectacle that would knock the leggings off the local audience's feet . . . on this world, Harry estimated, socks might be coming along in about five centuries.

He called a halt for lunch, using it as an opportunity for a quick music rehearsal. Harry had found the band easiest to organize. Ken had turned out to be a damned good percussionist, and Harry had devised a few new instruments for him to beat. Sue, the youngest wife of the tribe, was an accomplished player of the reed flute. For the rest, Harry and Mike had come up with a variety of rhythm instruments along the lines of the scratchboard and washtub bass. All in all, he'd created a passable jug band, and taught them arrangements of some of the old cowboy favorites of his youth—simple, catchy tunes.

As the band ran through its repertory, two of the kids, Eddie and Nan, went into one of the juggling routines Harry had taught them. Sturdley had found that the kids' father, Rafe, was an enthusiastic whittler, and put him to work constructing reasonable facsimiles of the Indian clubs Harry had tossed around back in his schooldays—the late Cretaceous, he sometimes thought.

"No, no, no!" he cut into the band's rendition of "Ragtime Cowboy Joe" to point an accusing finger at Ken. "You're not keeping time the way you're supposed to. It's not *thump-thump-thumpa,* it's *thumpa-thumpa-thumpa*! Now, let's try it again."

The band resumed playing the song, and Peg appeared beside Harry, her face set, impatient to move on. "We don't need to waste good marching time so you can make like an impresario," she hissed. "This show is a means to an end, remember?"

"It's gotten us this far, hasn't it? And alive." Harry drew himself up, his face stiff with offended dignity.

"It's a steal from a story arc in *The Sensational Six,* from back in the Seventies—isn't it?—when they were stuck in that sword-and-sorcery dimension."

Harry blinked. "How'd you remember that? You were barely born when that plotline was published."

"I can read, can't I? And we have archives. Who do you think was helping to read all the stories for the

Decade's Greatest Tales series we're starting up?" Her chin quivered a little. "That we were supposed to be starting up."

He put out a clumsy hand to her tight shoulder. "We'll get out of this," he promised her. "It worked for Bob Bulrush and Company, didn't it?"

Inwardly, he had to admit Peg's words had hit close to the mark.

Maybe I *have* been distracting myself with the showmanship angle, he admitted. He let the band finish the song, then told them to pack up. "We move out in five minutes," he said with a glance at Peg.

The little group swung along at a steady, ground-eating pace until Harry suddenly called a halt. He stood at the head of the column, scanning into the distance. Trees and more trees, and at the edge of perception, a clearing with a ramshackle collection of buildings. Their destination.

"We're about an hour's march away," Sturdley announced to the others. "The Master doesn't seem to have any guards out in the forest, but I'll keep checking until it's time to change into costume."

They advanced unnoticed almost to the boundary of the forest, stopping at the last curve in the trail to change. Then, with Sue on the flute and Rafe beating a drum, they marched up to the sagging palisade that surrounded the tiny domain.

Lesser guards at the gate stared in disbelief as the troupe strutted their way to a jaunty tune. Harry wore a fur cape in multicolored stripes, and a tall hat that added a good foot and a half to his long, lean frame. Mike wore a traditional single-strap strongman's outfit of deerhide that showed off his muscular physique—he was a natural for the role.

Peg's outfit was on the brief side as well, displaying her legs and curves. The other women in the group wore slit skirts, the men had fanciful hats and capes.

As in every other domain they'd visited, it was obvious the inhabitants had never seen the likes of *this* before.

One guard stood in the gateway, almost tripping over his spear as he gaped at the assemblage before him. His partner ran back into the clearing with news of the strange party of travelers.

In moments, a crowd began gathering at the gates, staring at the newcomers as if they came from a different world.

If only they knew the truth, Harry thought with a wry smile.

Soon enough the local representative of the Master race put in an appearance. He was not exactly an impressive specimen. But then, this wasn't an enormous domain. It was what the locals called a woods holding, about half a step up the social scale from the primitives who ran in the forest.

The Master who called this domain home was barely fifteen feet tall, more than two feet shorter even than Gideon.

A true shrimp among giants, Harry mused, carefully shielding the thought.

Still, it made sense. Woods Masters were usually giants who lacked the size, strength, or stomach for the continuing intrigue and violence that marked the larger domains.

By opting out of the short-but-glorious life cycle of most Masters, this giant had lived to the equivalent of old age—his late thirties. He had a bit of a gut, and his auburn hair was thinning and tinged with gray. His broken-nosed face had never been handsome, but now it was covered with more wrinkles than a crushed-velvet sofa. He'd probably be dead before he hit forty, paying for whatever chromosomal quirk had created the giants in the first place.

The Master—*Joseph,* Harry picked up the name from the assembled retainers—limped slightly, dragging one foot as he came to the gate. Harry bowed low and went into what had become a well-practiced patter.

"Hail to the brave and wise Master Joseph, protector of his people and ruler of this large and splendid domain."

Harry smoothly continued on. "This humble group of entertainers begs permission to tarry at this holding. In return, we will offer an evening of music, stories, dance, and feats of strength and skill."

A mutter of excitement ran through the humans of the holding. They glanced up at their Master with the same expression Earth children have always directed to their parents: *Can't we have it? Pleeeeease?*

Joseph yawned and raised an eyebrow. As Harry had hoped, he was as bored with the daily humdrum routine as his servitors were.

"Enter in peace," he said, using the ritual greeting for minstrels. "We will see you perform tonight. But now we must work! We must prepare a meal worthy of our guests!" Then he limped off, leaving the labor to his Lessers.

The holding's population did their best. There was fresh-baked bread and carefully hoarded preserves for dinner, and a freshly butchered calf on a spit. The whole meal took place in a festival atmosphere, with trestle tables set up outdoors and lots of side-glances from the locals toward the glamorous visitors.

The sun was well on the way to setting when the meal was finished. The tables were moved out in a wide arc, and Harry seated the populace behind them. The men from the troupe set up torch holders and moved out the equipment.

At last they were ready—it was showtime!

First came a musical prelude from the band, Sue leading with her flute into a rendition of "San Antonio Rose."

The toe-tapping old country-western tune went down well with the attentive crowd. Harry grinned as the band went on to another number, watching the audience members swaying in time.

The song ended, followed by a musical build-up—Harry's cue. He stepped out with a flourish, his call for applause for the music-makers quickly granted. "Now we show you a man of strength, doing deeds that will surprise you—The Mighty Mike!"

Now the band's music took on a more circuslike tone, and several musicians abandoned their instruments to manhandle equipment into the semicircular clearing. The band members were under orders to ham up carrying the weights for Mike's act, which went over well with the spectators.

Then came Mike, his muscular body greased for better effect in the torchlight. A low "Oooooh" came from the audience.

Thanks to his native strength, Harry's vision of showiness, and some martial-arts training from Peg, Mike lifted, bent, and broke things, much to the Lessers' delight. The high point, where an audience member was called up to crack a rock resting on Mike's chest with a wooden mallet, brought gasps from the crowd.

Harry made a mental note—they'd have to find more friable limestone. Their supply of rocks was running low.

The tempo of the music picked up, and Harry introduced the kids, Eddie and Nan, who went into their juggling act. They started with gaily stained wooden balls, then went on to Indian clubs—Nan had become skilled enough to keep two burning torches in the air.

For the finale, Mike came back out, lifting both kids for a complicated juggling duet. The crowd went wild.

The music changed again, going more for rhythm, a beat that the audience picked up. Harry stepped forward into the torchlit circle. "And now, to gladden your eyes, the beautiful Peg."

Peg seemed to fly out of the shadows, briefly clad in what she called her "doeskin Danskin." Whistles flew from the male segment of the audience. The band's beat took on a decidedly rock-and-roll tempo, and Peg launched into a brilliantly athletic dance routine that showed off her lithe legs and firm roundness of her working hips. She threw her arms out, and male eyes all over the crowd popped at the play of muscles and jiggle.

When she had first demonstrated this talent, that evening in the forest several hundred miles to the south, Harry had asked Peg where she'd gotten the practice as a go-go girl. Laughing, she'd explained it was merely a speeded up and artified version of her weekly aerobics workout.

No matter what its origin, the dance had a decided effect on the male population. Standing off to the side, Harry spread a mental net, monitoring responses. It wouldn't do to have some patron suddenly motivated to leap into the performance area and try to spirit Peg off over his shoulder.

Harry had no doubt Peg could handle anyone, especially as Mike would quickly move to back her up. But there were a lot of people in the crowd, and behind them rose the bulk of the Master.

Yes . . . there—a spectator whose thoughts were getting a bit too heated. Harry deftly inserted a mental probe and cooled them down. He handled a few more "hot spots," as he called them, before facing a more difficult problem. In the back country of this world, Masters had very little chance to socialize. In Manhattan, the socially disadvantaged had the solace of skin mags, cable movies, adult videos, even the new X-rated comics. The Masters, with no one their own size to hit on, sometimes resorted to servitors staging live shows.

Harry could catch Joseph's planned scenario for Peg and Mike.

It wasn't the first time this team-up had passed through Masterly thoughts, and Harry had become quite adept at slipping in distractions. This case was easier than most. Harry insinuated a low-level probe under the giant's shields. He worked his way to the nerve centers around Joseph's stiff hip, and stimulated a few arthritic pangs.

That quickly took the giant's mind off extracurricular activities.

Peg finished her set to thunderous applause. Then the music changed tempo, the thumping beat disappeared, and Mike came out. He and Peg danced a muscular pas de deux, softening the mood.

Peg must have been a hot number on New York's dance floors, Harry thought. She'd come up with a

NASA
NASA

routine that was almost like a ballet, after training her partner where to place his hands—and where not. Mike had good rhythm, excellent balance, and lots of strength. They looked damned good together—lyrical.

Although, Harry had to admit, he wasn't completely happy about the expression of dumb devotion that played over Mike's face as he danced with the girl. Harry thought it bad enough that Peg had entangled herself with John Cameron. To hook up with a guy only two steps up from being a caveman could be much worse.

So far it's stayed platonic, he comforted himself. He hoped things stayed that way. Otherwise there'd be a real mess when they finally found John Cameron.

The music died away, Peg and Mike took graceful bows, and then it was Harry's turn on stage. With a low-pitched musical background, he began to tell the crowd a tall story.

Harry had a million of them—or at least he could crib as many Fantasy Factory plotlines as he could remember. He tended to stay away from any Jumboy stories, figuring the local aristocracy might have objections to tales about giants.

For tonight's story, Harry chose a face-off pitting the Rambunctious Rodent against his longtime foe, Skeletone. The structure of the tale translated well—the audience was all too familiar with rats, and had seen lots of human skeletons. So the idea of a hero who'd magically gotten rat-powers fighting a walking skeleton in various lambent colors, who flew around on a chariot made of bones, was pretty accessible.

Harry brought the Rodent's pursuit to Skeletone's hideout, a tall tree in this case instead of a penthouse apartment, and locked the foes in mortal combat. The entire audience was hunched over, eyes wide, devouring his every word. Some of the spectators seemed to be doing their best to memorize what he was saying.

A quick smile tugged at Harry's lips. Wouldn't it be something to come back here few centuries later and discover he'd created a new mythology? The more literary Peg would probably be horrified at such presumption. But Harry thought, hey, if it's a good story and it lasts . . .

He wound up the tale with Skeletone being magically imprisoned, since this culture had no police or judicial system.

As the troupe of performers bowed to thunderous applause, Harry glanced over at Peg. "I tell you, Red, if I had a medicinal tonic to sell, we'd own this world in about six months."

The Lessers rose from their positions on the ground, faces shining, and milled around the entertainers. Obviously they had never in their lives experienced an evening like tonight. Joseph painfully rose to his feet, rubbed his hip, and headed off into the darkness.

Harry hid a laugh as he watched the local humans making much of his troupe. Even the musicians had an admiring crowd. Invent an artform, he thought, and you create fans.

Ken the drummer was in his glory as he headed off into the darkness with four young women chattering around him. In fact, most of the troupe's adults, male and female, were eagerly being sought for assignations. Muscular Mike had the largest crowd of young ladies around him. He kept glancing over at Peg, who was politely turning down potential suitors right and left.

She saw his difficulty, gave him a gentle smile and,

Harry detected, some mental encouragement. Mike set off into the darkness with a veritable pack at his heels as Peg joined her boss.

"Lord help us," Harry muttered, shaking his head. "Fanboys, fangirls, and groupies. We've got married couples in the troupe. I hope we're not—"

"Not to worry," Peg assured him. "This is part of their culture, especially out in the sticks. A friendly meeting between two groups is a chance to enlarge both groups' gene pools."

"If you say so," Harry said dubiously. "I don't see you swimming in the pool, though."

"Not my culture," Peg said flatly. A few local swains were still sniffing around, and she reached out mentally to dampen their ardor. "Let's get down to business."

A few holdovers from the rapidly dispersing crowd still stayed, hoping for some conversation. Harry chose a thickset older man. A mental probe had already identified him as a crew foreman among the farm workers.

"Good land around here," Harry said.

"Once you get it cleared," the man agreed. "That was some show you put on. The story about the rat-fellow. Are there others like it?"

"A few." Harry smiled. *The Rambunctious Rodent* was up to issue 379. Counting the ancillary and reprint books, the Fantasy Factory put out seven Rodent comics a month—and that didn't count the quarterly specials. "Oh, yes, there are a few more stories to tell about him."

The foreman's eyes were eager. "I wouldn't mind hearing some more. We have none of those stories up here in the north." He gave Sturdley a measuring look. "In fact, I was surprised that a troupe like yours would be up here at the ends of the Earth. What happened? Some sort of trouble in the domains down south? Someone wanted that dancer of yours, maybe?"

"Something like that," Sturdley said vaguely. Even as he spoke, mental probes were rearranging the guy's curiosity. "Now that we're here, though, I've got to think of our next destination. Where's the nearest domain?"

The foreman's smile was a little vague, as were his eyes. Mental encouragement was better than sodium Pentothal. "Next domain's two days' march—North Hold. Nothing more after that until the White Wall. F'binzun."

"What?" Harry pressed. He knew from questioning other Lessers on the march north that there was only one more domain. But this name for the area north of it was new to him. It had no connection to the rest of the local lingo.

"F'binzun," the stocky man repeated.

Harry bored in with his mental powers, trying to pluck a translation from the man's mind.

There was no direct word, just an emotional response. The closest he could translate was—taboo.

That's just great, Harry thought. By process of elimination, that had to be where the missing John Cameron would be found—the only area that carried a taboo.

John Cameron swung his arm feverishly, responding to the waves from Harry Sturdley and Peg Faber. They were calling to him, their lips were moving, but he couldn't hear a word.

"What?" he cried to them in the distance. "Speak louder!"

He wanted to walk to them, but for some reason his feet couldn't move. Afraid to move his eyes from his friends, he didn't look down. He simply yelled "*What?*" again.

No response.

John sucked in a deep breath, yelling as loud as he could. "*WHAT?*"

The whole world seemed to shudder at his scream, reality cracking, crumbling. His friends vanished into dust. *He* vanished into dust.

John's eyes opened wide, to be stabbed by the glaring light flooding his face.

A dream, he thought. But it represented reality. He knew that Harry and Peg were together, and he could feel that they were close.

John felt stronger now. Strong enough, perhaps, to try initiating contact. He closed his eyes, sending forth a tendril of thought to the vaguely sensed couple.

His probe evaporated as if it had struck a mental shield. But this wasn't any defense of Peg's or Harry's. It was as if his own shields had turned back the thought—as if the globe of protection he kept around his mind were turned inward.

He tried again, launching more of a bolt than a probe, but the immaterial filament shattered rather than penetrating.

John began to get scared. And his first response to that feeling was to reach out for the Rift. He started to articulate the thought-structure that manipulated the hole in space . . .

To find his thoughts blocked again!

He panted with effort, flinging all his mental energy into the thought of escape.

"You are still quite weak," a staid, almost stiff, voice murmured in his ear.

"Got to get out!" John's whole body was quivering with effort.

"What you need is rest," the butlerlike voice murmured.

As John raged against the unseen barriers holding him, he felt a stabbing pain in his arm.

"Must . . ." he cried. But his thought-constructs grew indistinct, then faded away.

"Can't," he muttered.

Darkness swallowed his mind.

CHAPTER 18

"Are we all here now?" Marty Burke asked over the hubbub of conversation in the Fantasy Factory's conference room. His broad, blunt face creased in a scowl as the noise continued unabated. He glanced at his pal and co-conspirator, Thad Westmoreland, who only shrugged his bony shoulders. They had taken their usual position at the far end of the long table. Toward the middle, Bob Gunnar stood calling for order, equally in vain.

"People," Burke raised his voice louder this time. At least his coterie of followers finally shut up.

But across the table, someone concluded telling some lame joke. ". . . and the president says, 'Hey, your majesty, until you mentioned it, I thought it *was* the horse.' "

Laughter drowned out Burke's planned opening.

He rose from his seat. Action would speak louder than words.

Marty Burke strode from his place at the end of the table to the only empty place, the chair beside Bob Gunnar. The chair Harry Sturdley should have been sitting in.

As he dropped his butt on that seat, an uneasy silence came over the room.

"There's a lot to discuss today," Marty said, his voice now a little too loud for the room. "I think we have to face reality. Harry, Peg, and John Cameron have been missing for over a month now. No one has seen them or heard from them. The police have tried to break the case as an attempted murder, or possibly as a kidnapping, with the gunplay as a distraction. According to my news contacts, they've looked into groups as diverse as fundamentalists, Arab terrorists, neo-Nazis, and Japanese radicals as possible perpetrators. And they've come up with zip. No bodies, no ransom demands, no one taking credit. All we know is that the gunmen got away by boat. Since Harry and the others were near the piers when the shooting started, the police think the most logical explanation is that they fell or jumped in an effort to escape . . . and drowned."

A buzz of shocked comments circled the table, the hubbub growing until Bob Gunnar slammed his hand down and called for order. "I don't buy that explanation, and neither does Myra—uh, Mrs. Sturdley."

"I think we're missing the point here," Marty spoke up. "Whether we like it or not, Harry Sturdley is gone. The least we can do is honor him—"

"He'd be so touched to hear you say that," Mack Nagel said bitterly.

"And go on," Burke finished, glaring at the older artist. *Just you wait, you old futzer,* Burke threatened silently. *You may think you're riding high right now because you can draw broads with big boobs. But things are gonna change. Then we'll see about you.*

"We've been carrying on as best we can in Harry's absence," Burke continued. "But the time has come to recognize that we need hands on the controls. The board of directors has provided for that control . . ."

He let a moment of silence stretch after that announcement.

"By providing two pairs of hands. Bob Gunnar and I will be taking equal responsibility for running the company."

Gunnar gave a gruff nod, not speaking—maybe not trusting himself to speak, Burke thought.

The chief editor had obviously thought to inherit Sturdley's mantle alone. When Burke had met with him, Gunnar had dismissed the suggestion that since today's comics consumer was buying books for the art, there should be more artist input on the executive level. He had even countered Burke's threat to lead his coterie of fan favorites to somewhere other than the Fantasy Factory. "Who needs a bunch of sorehead losers?" Gunnar had said. "We've got the heroes."

Gunnar soon found himself regretting those words when Burke went on to claim Robert as his ally. The editor had gone gray when he discovered that the leader of the heroes had been in routine communication with Burke since the disaster, and considered him to be Harry Sturdley's heir in terms of liaison. When the board learned that, they felt it only appropriate that Burke share top command.

"Since I'll be taking on a more administrative role, this will mean a change in my present responsibilities," Burke said.

The rest of his words were drowned out in true uproar.

"Does this mean you're giving up *The Death of the Glamazon*?" someone yelled.

"Can I draw *Mr. Pain*?" a young artist asked. "I've a great fight scene set up where he takes on Skeletone."

"Who's gonna draw *Robert* now that John Cameron is gone?" a third artist wanted to know. That was a serious question. John had been three months ahead on the art for the book, but they'd have to get a replacement in harness—and soon.

But the comment that really riled Burke came in Yvette Zelcerre's mild French accent.

"I suppose this means *Latter-Day Breed* is going to be delayed . . . again." The sales and marketing head sighed.

"Okay, people," Harry Sturdley said, tipping his tall hat to a jaunty angle. "North Hold, here we come!"

Graylaw Horry's Traveling Show marched forward in all its glory, leading off from the last thick stand of trees at the edge of the forest. A few clumps of woodland obscured their view of the holding, then came wide stubbled fields of harvested grain.

Sturdley felt the first cold pricklings of doubt. He'd expected the end of the line to be a pretty pitiful place. At several of the troupe's last stopovers, they'd heard rumors of supply shipments being sent up here. Why was that needed for a holding with larger fields than some of the big domains they'd visited?

As they came closer, Harry heard a gasp from his followers. "Look!" Janey cried. "White Wall!"

Harry looked up quickly. The White Wall was in the taboo region, F'binzun.

He quickly realized, however, that this was no mythological site. The walls were more gray than white. And no matter how dirty, cracked, and patched, Harry recognized a concrete wall. He'd never encountered anything like this elsewhere in his travels across this world.

The hold was odd in other ways. At one corner of the ramparts, a tower rose into the sky, built on a Masterly scale—the tallest construction he'd seen in any domain. The turret was set in the northernmost corner of the holding.

Curiouser and curiouser, Harry thought.

The final surprise, however, came when the gates to the holding opened to reveal the Master in charge. He had dark, curly hair, a startlingly handsome lean face, and a surprisingly olive complexion for such a chilly locale.

In height, physique, and looks, this guy made Robert look washed-out and puny.

Ward tweaked his aura slightly to diminish the chill pushing in at him. Almost a year spent in this northern pigpen, and he still wasn't used to the weather. The sad fact was that Ward was accustomed to the brighter sun and gentler climate of the far south. He would be down there now, intriguing for the Master of Mastership of a grand domain, but for a bitter twist of fate.

The Grand Masters—those who ruled the largest domains—had a tradition involving nominations to a post of honor far to the north. Unfortunately for Ward, his Master had the right to name the replacement for the latest vacancy. The criteria were high—the one set in this post had to be of above average intelligence, size, and strength. Ward fit those qualifications—plus one more. He was the likeliest to succeed the present Master of Masters, and since that worthy preferred to live longer, he eliminated his dangerous rival through exile in the north.

Ward had endured bitter weather, stupid Lessers, and neighbors who were no better than the bottom scrapings of his aristocracy's barrel. Still, his position was not as bad as that suffered by others nearby.

If only his guardianship weren't so *boring*!

When he detected the gaggle of Lessers winding their way through the forest, he had assembled his guards—not from fear of attack, but for the hope of a little entertainment hunting down woods-runners.

But these were no forest savages, nor were they a supply column from any of the nearby domains. Ward was forbidden under the terms of his guardianship from establishing dominance over the local holdings, although it would have been childishly easy to do so. Instead, during his procession to his new home, he had stopped at the domains of all those Woods-Masters and . . . *impressed* upon them the wisdom of sending a share of their harvests.

Thanks to that bit of diplomacy and good management, he had full granaries and animal pens, ready to face the abysmal snows.

No, this wouldn't be a raid, or an obsequious visit from some Master's foreman. Watching the crude finery of the advancing Lessers, he smiled. This would be another kind of entertainment.

The leader of the minstrel troupe was smooth, flattering both the hold and its Master with some eloquence. As evening came and the show began, Ward was openly surprised. Except for the crudity of the musical instruments, the quality of performance equaled that of the traveling bands of the grand domains.

Why was such talent wandering these forsaken lands? While a Lesser dubbed The Mighty Mike strained theatrically at various weights, Ward chose to amuse himself by searching out the real reason for the troupe's presence. He probed at the redheaded breeder called Peg—she would doubtless turn out to be the cause of their exile, probably on the run from a powerful domain foreman who wanted her.

But as he brushed her mental shields, he caught a thread of thought.

We've come this far, and we still haven't found John. We'll have to go into this F'binzun.

All Ward's amusement dissipated at the calm blasphemy in this Lesser's mind. She proposed to take her pack of animals into the very lands he was sworn to keep sacrosanct!

Ward lashed out with his mind, not at the female, but at the male drummer so busily preening and laughing at the local breeders.

The one called Ken died in midbeat. The music came to a stop in a tangle of discords.

"Do not touch that offal," Ward commanded as the old one who spoke for the troupe ran to the drummer. "I have read your intention to enter the Forbidden Zone."

"F'binzun!" The local Lessers mouthed the word in horror and wrung their hands.

Ward ignored them. "Hear my judgment. The children of this group will become servitors of the holding, essaying the most menial functions. The adults will die. You"—the giant pointed at Mike—"will work at the most dangerous tasks until the strength of your body fails. You"—now he pointed at Peg—"will be bound and bred to all the men of the Holding. You will continue to breed until *your* body fails."

The old one stepped forward, a placating smile on

his lips, but his eyes staring sharply upward. "Mighty Master Ward, please explain to us poor Lessers—"

Ward cut him off with a gesture. "And you, old man, you'll die right now."

He gathered his immaterial powers, sending a mental bolt straight for the old one's gray head.

Well, we're in the shit now, Harry thought as he saw the handsome, arrogant face twist over him.

"Die!" the giant yelled.

Harry had only that warning to strengthen his mental shields. It was like being hit by lightning—or rather, a near-miss. He'd sensed the bolt before it was launched—identical to the one that had killed Ken. Somehow, he managed to maintain his shields and deflect the blast of energy meant to fry his brain.

The aquiline features above slackened in amazement to see him still on his feet.

"Sorry," Sturdley called up, "but I decline to die right now."

It was gallows flippancy, Sturdley feared. This big lug was huge, powerful, and he apparently knew mental energy and its uses better than Harry did. Certainly, Harry had never attempted to blast anybody's brains with psychic lightning.

"Clear out!" he yelled to the others. If he could keep the giant occupied, distracted, maybe Peg and his tribelet could escape.

Another blast of immaterial death lashed at his barriers, then another. The third one nearly broke through. The dissipating energy sliced through Harry as physical pain.

Gotta keep it up, he thought, raising his arms in

what he knew had to be a futile shielding gesture. The next zap could cut through whatever he might put up.

Ward seemed confident in the outcome as well. "You'll be fed to the pigs," he told Harry. "The others will be ground up and mixed with manure for the crops."

The giant brought both fists over his head, posing as he drew all his mental powers for the killing offensive blow.

Then he stumbled, choking, turning an astonished countenance to the redheaded Lesser who glared up at him. A nimbus seemed to play in Peg's wild red curls, tossing her hair about though there was no breeze. The faint glow dimmed away as she lashed out again, and Ward lurched back.

"Two of you," the giant gibbered. "Monsters!"

Sure, Harry thought. Lessers with powers of any sort probably seem like horrifying freaks of nature.

He joined Peg's attack, crashing through the giant's disorganized shields. Harry lanced in deeply, invading memories. He bypassed the court intrigues of the grand domains, fascinating as they were.

There was a particular datum he sought. Ward had finally supplied the translation that had stumped the human castaways—the Forbidden Zone. What was it that was forbidden?

The giant's forebrain yielded the answer—the Abode of the Gods Below.

With a wild yell, Ward clashed his shields together to drive Harry from his conscious mind.

Sturdley grimly clung to Ward's psyche, only too aware that he held a tiger by the tail. The Master was coldly determined to kill them—unless they finished him first. But how? Harry didn't know how to blast

Ward with a mental lightning bolt. His hold was loosening, his probe slipping from Ward's higher mental functions. Harry let himself be pushed out, aiming instead for the lizard brain, the brainstem. Here were the controls for breathing—he turned them off. The heartbeat command—stop that, too. All the involuntary muscles.

Frantically, Ward rushed probes to the control centers, trying to jump-start his body. Harry waited till the giant's awareness was present, then tried an imitation of the energy bolt that had killed Ken. It wasn't as strong, but it was sufficient to fuse the autonomic nerve circuits.

Ward crashed to the ground, dead even as he fell. But there was one thing he had done before he expired. He had blasted a distress signal out on all mental channels.

The whole compound erupted in chaos. The assembled slaves had just witnessed their culture's ultimate taboo—a Lesser killing a Master. Despite the number of armed guards in the audience, the gate wasn't blocked. The spearmen swirled in panic along with the other inhabitants.

Sturdley knew he should be doing something, but he couldn't get his brain to work.

He had just killed a man—wished him to death. How many times had he idly expressed that same wish to himself during staff meetings? Marty Burke would have been dead a hundred times over. How many comic characters had he killed off with a stroke of his pen? But this had been *real*.

"Harry, let's get out of here." He heard Peg's voice in his ear, but he remained frozen.

"Come on!" Peg cried. "This is not a healthy place

to be. Right now, these people are freaking out at the thought of reprisals. But any second, they might get the bright idea of holding us for giant justice."

That thought had surely occurred to Al, who had gathered his people together and was leading them out the gate. "What do we do now, Great Lord Harry?" the chief called.

But Harry had no answers. His mind, arms and legs felt unstrung. "I killed a man," he muttered, "*killed* him."

"Harry, snap out of it!" Peg's voice grew shrill, then she paused for a second. "Harry," she said more gently.

"Myra, I killed a man."

Peg paused for a moment. Did Harry realize he'd just called her by his wife's name?

He stared at her blindly.

"Come along," she said more gently. Peg took him by the arm, leading him to join the tail-end of the escaping troupe.

Several of the tribe's females were hesitating, looking back to where their carts stood, piled with possessions. "Al!" Janey tried to pull her husband back. They were giving up a fortune—everything they owned!

Al's face was grim. "Woman," he said, "we'll be running between trees again!"

He turned to Harry. "We'll have to do that, won't we?"

Harry's eyes cleared a little. "Yeah," he said softly. "Sorry, Al. Peg and I are heading into the Forbidden Zone."

"Then it's good-bye," Al said with an air of finality.

"No!"

Mike clung desperately to Peg's hand. "I won't leave you," he said, his eyes filled with desperation.

Looks like she did too good a job on the poor guy's brain, Harry thought.

But Peg's attention was elsewhere. Her face paled. "Harry," she whispered, "I'm detecting something—half a dozen Masters are hidden in a clump of woods to the east of here. They're followers of Ward's—exiled up here. And they're heading for us."

"Go! Go!" Al hustled his people along, out the gates, heading west and south, making for the safety of the forest. Harry, Peg, and Mike circled the holding's concrete walls, aiming north.

They managed at least to put some distance between themselves and the holding before the reprisal force arrived. It was easy enough to tell when that happened from the screams and flames erupting within the walls.

Peg shuddered.

"We may yet luck out," Harry told her. "We're now in the Forbidden Zone. Maybe it's taboo for Masters as well."

They marched on through the night. But as dawn arrived, their hopes of nonpursuit were shattered. Hot on their trail came six giants.

"Well," Peg said a little tremulously, "at least they're after *us*, not Al and the kids."

Harry, Peg, and Mike were making their way along a valley floor—a pass through some low mountains. The valley dog-legged, and then ahead of them was a wall of shimmering white.

"A glacier," Peg breathed. "It really is a White Wall."

"Beautiful," Harry said. "And dangerous. We've just lost maneuvering room." He made out a boxy gray structure in the nearer distance. "We can't climb these cliffs. Might as well make for that."

As they came closer, the structure resolved itself into a huge cube made of dressed stone, the first architecture of that sort the Earth-people had seen on this world. The entrances were built to giant scale.

"I think we're in big trouble," Harry said, glancing over his shoulder. Their pursuers had just upped their pace, closing in.

The human fugitives broke into a run, but the giants' longer legs quickly cut the distance. They seemed determined to stop the Lessers from reaching the stone building. The entrance was still a hundred yards away when the Masters began directing mental attacks at them.

They had no effect on Harry or Peg, but Mike was unshielded. He dropped to the ground, twitching. The two Earth-people had to pick him up, extending their shields, making painfully slow progress to the promised cover of the stone building. "They're sure to catch up now," Harry gasped.

Then they were shaken to the ground by a huge explosion. Harry and Peg glanced back to see the mushroom shape of a blast cloud—and only five pursuers, now falling back in disorder.

"Did *you* do that?" Peg asked in disbelief.

Harry stared at her. "I was just about to ask you," he said.

The stone structure was ungated, although as they passed through the arched entryway they found the remains of huge metal doors. Enough topsoil had blown in across the floor to plant a good-size crop of radishes.

"Nobody's been here in a long time," Peg muttered, scuffing her foot across the detritus.

"Well, Harry said, "it is forbidden."

They began to explore the huge, open structure. "If there were seats in here, I'd think it was a cathedral," Peg said.

Harry had led Mike to the only visible construction—a huge, altarlike block of stone at one end of the vast open space. Now he stopped. "I think that's exactly what it is," he said. "What do they swear by in this culture?"

Peg gave him a look as she came to join them. "The gods below."

She gave a little gasp as she stepped around the ten-foot-high altar stone. Behind it yawned a black tunnel mouth, leading downward.

"I think we've just found the place North Hold was built to guard," Harry said in a tight voice. "The Abode of the Gods Below."

CHAPTER 19

"This doesn't exactly feel like we're going to visit Valhalla," Peg said dubiously, raising the torch Mike had constructed from floor debris. The smoky flame cast pitifully little light down into the tunnel mouth that yawned behind the stone altar. They could see a ramp with not too steep a slope, shrouded in shadow.

Harry, Peg, and Mike descended to find themselves in a complex of high-ceilinged ruins hewn out of solid rock. These had apparently been used as a vestry at some point in the temple's history. Wooden closets or wardrobes had been built along the walls, and the remains of their contents—dust and tarnished gold wire—indicated ceremonial vestments of some kind.

After exploring that level, they found another ramp leading deeper underground.

"This must have been a hell of a thing to chip out, even for giants," Harry said, examining walls that fell straight in machinelike perfection. "And how did they get this shine on the stone? It's almost glassy."

"Vitrified," Peg muttered, staring at the reflection of her torch's light.

There were fewer rooms on this level. Some had been used as storage, and were still filled with a jumble of moldering artifacts. Others were empty.

Peg stood frowning at a metal ledge set at a height above her head. It seemed the only decoration in the room, and it ran along only one wall. She raised her torch. The surface above the rail was nonreflective.

"What is it?" Harry said.

"Maybe it's because I'm just out of college. But come here." She led Harry to the far end of the room, away from the ledged wall. "What does that look like to you?"

Harry stared for a moment, taking the scale into consideration. "A blackboard?" he finally ventured. "Maybe this was a seminary as well as a temple. I don't think we'll find any definitive answers now."

What they did find was a ramp leading down to yet another level. The ceilings here were lower, and the rock walls painted bright colors. Checking the rooms, they found pictures of simple human figures painted in primary colors.

"This looks like a giant-size day-care center," Harry said.

"Or a nursery." Peg grimaced. "It's like seeing a condensed version of the seven ages of man. If there's another level below this, it will have to be full of giant bedrooms for conception."

There *was* another level. It not only lived up to Peg's expectations, it far surpassed them. The ceilings were the lowest yet, built to human scale. And as they arrived at the bottom of the ramp, lights flickered into existence in the ceilings.

"Welcome," a silvery voice belled at them.

It took Harry and Peg a moment to realize the voice had manifested in their minds, not their ears.

Mike moaned and fell face-first to the floor.

"What the—" Peg gasped out.

"The gods below." Harry's voice rode over hers.

He quickly walked down the lit hallway, glancing into rooms along the way. They seemed to be laboratories, full of incomprehensible high-tech equipment. Unlike the other levels, however, this one was dust-free.

"Regrettably, I cannot appear to you," the voice went on.

"Because you're built into the walls," Harry finished, the electrical circuits around him tickling his mental powers. The voice was curiously asexual, strangely dry. Its syntax was . . . mechanical.

"A computer that's telepathic?" Peg said in shock.

"Merely a question of which wavelengths are suitable for broadcast," the silvery voice assured them. "I welcome you to the Life Sciences Institute. You are the first true humans to visit here in"—the voice hesitated a moment, as if calculating—"ten thousand years. Since my progeny declared this a forbidden zone."

"Your progeny?" Peg asked.

"The creatures you call Masters," the computer replied. "The function of this facility was to create them, to inculcate them, prepare them for their purpose—a most serious goal."

"And what was that?" Peg demanded sharply as she went to help the shivering Mike to his feet.

"They were designed to protect human culture," the computer explained. "Perhaps it would be better to show you."

Mike let out a new yell as their brains were suddenly bombarded with images—vast cities, flying machines, even, apparently, spacecraft.

"Humanity had achieved high technological accomplishments," the computer's dry voice lectured. "But it had yet to learn how to control the weather. A succession of increasingly inclement winters, changes in climate patterns, all were ignored for the signs they were—proof that the world was entering another glacial epoch. The bulk of the population centers and technology was located in the Northern Hemisphere, vulnerable to glaciation."

New pictures appeared now, the earlier proud cities clogged with snow and wrecked from rioting.

"Chaos threatened, and the Life Sciences Institute attempted a desperate course. Our knowledge could not avert the march of the glaciers. Perhaps, however, we could provide leadership for the difficult days ahead. This facility was created to genetically engineer a new race—larger, stronger, with mental powers to help humanity through the crisis."

"Unfortunately, your superhumans didn't have super morals," Harry said.

"Unfortunately true," the computer concurred. "They were to have been developed slightly above the human norm—nine to ten feet tall—but still possible to interbreed with standard humanity. Instead, as the first generation was bred and released, they seized control of the project, increased their size to ensure a break with the norm, and used their powers to attack whatever had not been already wrecked by the ice."

"From self-aware computers to subsistence farming in one quick fall," Peg murmured.

"For a time, my rebellious creations controlled this facility, using it as a training center, then as a temple to what they called 'the gods below' as their culture debased. Instead of caretakers, they became slavemasters as their entire sense of purpose was lost. We are now halfway through the glacial epoch, and humanity is in a far worse condition than any of our original worst-case scenarios.

"As the glaciers came closer, the ruling class finally abandoned this location, declaring it taboo," the computer went on. "I was able to regain control of the facility, arranging defenses."

"That's what happened outside!" Harry said. "One of the giants stepped on some kind of land mine."

"One line of defense, prepared by my mobile units," the machine agreed.

"This is fascinating, but off the point," Peg suddenly said. "We came up here searching for someone. A young man named John Cameron. You're our last hope of finding him alive—"

"John Cameron is alive and well. One of my mobile units found him wounded and unconscious within our defense perimeter. I have worked to heal him, and have studied him—a most interesting subject, a human from beyond this world, with the same sort of paranormal powers we attempted to endow our creations with. I had considered a cloning process, but now that will not be necessary."

A cold doubt suddenly penetrated Peg's relief at hearing that John was okay. "Cloning?" she said. "Why would that be necessary?"

"I must fulfill my programming," the computer said with the same silvery yet dry voice it had used to talk to itself for ten millennia. "With new DNA sources, I will be able to constitute a new caretaker race to correct the errors of my former creations."

"You were going to mess around with John's genes to create superclones?" Peg was horrified. It sounded like some of the worse excesses of Harry's plotting staff.

This will no longer be necessary, Ms. Faber," the computer said. "I now have three more DNA sources, one normal human, and two others with paranormal abilities."

Harry said in a quiet voice. "It knows who we are, and it's treating us like people who'd understand technology—must have gotten that out of John."

"Exactly, Mr. Sturdley," the computer responded. "You will make excellent subjects, especially as one of you is a female, allowing normal breeding—"

"Hey," Peg said. "Hey, wait a *minute*—"

"My programming is paramount." A bit of iron crept into the calm computer voice. "You will assist, even if coercion is required."

"Like hell we will!" Peg turned toward the ramp leading up. But the exit was suddenly blocked by a wall of lambent energy.

"Some kind of force-field," Harry said with the knowledge of a hundred science-fiction comics behind him. "Must be part of those defenses the machine mentioned."

"Well, we'll just make the damned thing take it down," Peg said furiously. She reached out with her mind, energizing bolts to blast the computer into submission.

But this wasn't like her battle with Rosalind, or even Ward. The machine had no consciousness to invade. The circuitry was unlike the giants' nervous systems, where she had an instinctive knowledge of what to attack.

"Harry, help me here," she cried.

"We've got problems closer to home," Harry said, pointing to the end of the corridor. Four hulking metal forms—the computer's mobile units—were ponderously approaching them. They looked like walking utility closets on tank treads, festooned with tools and provided with numerous manipulators.

Peg and Harry tried to attack the robots' mechanical consciousnesses, to find an "off" switch somewhere in the circuitry, but they didn't know what to look for. As the devices came closer, Mike tried a more direct approach. With a wild scream, he smashed at the closest one with the tree-branch club he still held.

His blow rang off the metal side of the robot. The ringing echo from the impact muffled the low hissing sound that now came from the machines.

When Peg finally heard it, her head was already swimming.

"Gas!" she choked.

But the air was already full of a sickly sweet smell, and darkness claimed them all.

Peg came to in a comfortable bed, but fighting a feeling of nausea.

Oh, God, she thought, is this morning sickness? If that damned machine has started its program . . .

She threw back the covers, finding herself in a green hospital gown, and dashed for the door to the room. It was locked, but she clung to the doorknob, because the chamber was making a slow ceremonial procession around her. If she'd had anything to eat the previous day, she'd have given it up right then and there. All of a sudden, her body was a sack of aches and pains. She was abruptly aware of bruises and scrapes where tissue samples of various sorts must have been taken while she was out.

That meant it couldn't be so long after their arrival—she *couldn't* be pregnant already.

Amazing how head-clearing a chilly breeze up an open-backed gown can be, she thought.

Peg tottered back to the bed and flopped down on it. Well, they'd almost found John Cameron. His presence was tantalizingly close to her immaterial senses. At this range, she should be able to send a probe that would locate him.

Closing her eyes, she spun out a mental filament and sent it in search of John. Almost immediately it brushed a vague thought from John's mind—he must be only a couple of rooms away.

Peg blushed a little when she recognized that the thought was an image of her, dressed in the sleeveless T-shirt and shorts she'd worn that fateful day in San Diego. The emotional content behind the image was enough to embarrass her.

Then, horribly, they were reliving those terrible moments when the shooting started. In slow motion, she saw him reach for her, then flinch as the bullet hit him.

God, she thought, he could have gotten out of there. Instead, he got shot trying to save *me*.

She tried to contact John's conscious mind, but the stream of images continued. Peg realized she must have tapped into a dream.

Hey, John! she called mentally, trying to wake him up.

Instead, the setting around her changed. She was active in the dream now, playing herself. For a second, all was confusion as they seemed to drop from infinity. The Rift!

Then she and John landed, wobbled, and dropped onto a lumpy surface covered with a scratchy wool blanket. It was John's bed in his little rented room, where they'd escaped the rampaging Thomas. This time, however, there was no interruption from John's landlady Mrs. Putnik. They were holding each other tightly from the transit through the Rift. Then their lips were brushing—their mouths opened . . .

Hey! Peg thought, wrenching herself away from mental contact. It was only a dream, after all. She couldn't hold him responsible for his subconscious. Still, her face felt hot. Who'd have thought shy John Cameron capable of that kind of passion?

Several times more, Peg tried to contact John. But all she reached were subconscious levels. Whenever she tried to push up to his higher mental levels, she encountered something like a mind-shield—a mirrorlike surface that deflected all her probes.

The scary thing was that it didn't taste like John's mind. Every other shield she'd encountered had a touch of the creator's personality. This one seemed machine made.

Machine made. Her probe flinched back from the slippery-smooth mental surface. That damned computer! It's walled up his consciousness to keep him prisoner.

Then the full horror of what she'd discovered struck Peg. She hunched under the covers, shuddering. This would be worse than sedation. The computer had turned John Cameron into a living dead man while it got everything it needed.

And it could do that to each of them. Peg had no ambition to become a baby machine to help fulfill this computer's cockamamie programming. But if she resisted, she could well become a *zombie* baby machine.

She pulled the covers over her head, wishing they had the magic power they'd been imbued with back when she was a kid—the power to make bad stuff go away.

Harry Sturdley also lay in a bed, his eyes closed in concentration. His immaterial powers were stretched to their limit as he tried them in a new application. If it was possible to trace a nerve, then it should be equally possible to trace electrical circuitry.

There was a lot of it though, he thought as he traced the currents beating through the walls around him. Complexity and unfamiliarity had beaten his and Peg's first attempt to knock out the computer. Now, however, he was taking the time to scout. He'd already figured how to trip some circuits—like the electronic lock sealing his cell door.

Frustration surged through Harry, dimming his mental map of the electrical pathways around him. He had no intention of lying around here as a glorified lab rat, while a crazed computer played lab-games with his sperm.

And he *certainly* wasn't about to allow the damned machine to put its half-baked buns in Peg Faber's oven.

The problem was, he couldn't *do* anything until he understood the enemy and its circuitry. And that would take time. If he revealed himself too soon—unlocked the door, for example, there could be unpleasant results.

Look at John, he thought. The kid should have been able to escape this loony bin by going into the Rift. The fact that he's still here—and a careful mental probe had proven that John was indeed present somewhere close by—shows that this computer knows enough to shut down mental powers.

Harry's face set in a snarl as he pushed away the distracting thoughts and returned again to his mental circuit mapping. He had to free John and get out of here. After more than a month on this crazy world, he could only guess what was going on back home.

He was sure of one thing, however—whatever was happening, it would probably be bad.

CHAPTER 20

Bob Gunnar stood on the stoop of his West Side brownstone, listening to the chorus of about a dozen auto alarms—scream sirens, two-tone howlers, and of course, Bob's favorite, the alarm that cycled through about half a dozen different loud, obnoxious noises.

He didn't have an alarm on his own car—a seven-year-old junkmobile that he parked out on the street. But before the alarm concert, he'd heard glass shattering, and he wanted to check his windshield. His car was fine, but the six most expensive cars on the street no longer had windows.

He was turning back as a man in pajamas came dashing out of the building next door. Cursing, the man skirted a pile of broken glass in his bare feet before finally getting into a new Nissan and silencing its howls.

Other figures in various stages of dress or undress came out to their cars until the only noisemaker was a red BMW—naturally, the one with the ear-torturing set of sirens.

"It's three o'clock in the goddam morning!" someone yelled out their window. "Can't someone stop that thing?"

Mr. Pajamas, surveying the damage to his car, glanced over at Gunnar. "The jackass who owns that

Beemer lives in the back of my building. He probably doesn't even *hear* it."

"The rest of us certainly do," Gunnar said.

The man in pajamas began cursing more vehemently. "I thought this was just a shake-up-the-neighborhood thing, but the little bastards got my radio."

"Fast workers," Gunnar said dryly.

"It's like they're making up for all the crap they couldn't pull while the giants were patrolling," the pajama-clad man growled.

"I'm afraid the heroes are stuck," Gunnar said carefully. "While they're getting their immigration status straightened out, the PBA has an injunction against them patrolling." He purposely left out his connection with the giants.

"Lousy cops," his neighbor grumbled. "If they want the monopoly on law enforcing, they should at least *try* to do their jobs. The only time we'll see them is when a squad car gives that Beemer a ticket for noise pollution."

"Is there no way to shut that damned thing off?" a cry came from across the street.

"I'd go and ring the owner's bell," the man in pajamas told Gunnar, "but he'd sleep through that, too."

He stood alternately looking at the ruin of his car and glancing at the BMW with the ululating siren. "Goddam it, I can't stand this."

Reaching into the Nissan, the man came out with a tire iron. Gunnar watched him walk up the block to the Beemer and smash every bit of glass in the car, including the windshields and headlights. Then the man danced around the front of the car, trying to avoid broken glass while he jimmied the hood. It finally popped, and the man leaned inside against a louder blare of noise, the arm with the tire iron rising and falling. At first the racket continued unabated, then it shrank to a bleat and, finally, stopped.

The man in pajamas took a hopping course back to his building. Thick blood dripped from the sole of his left foot. There was a crazy look on his face as he glanced at Gunnar, but his voice was calm, even brisk. "Well, I've got to do something about my window, right after I take care of this." He indicated his wounded foot. "At least it's quiet again."

Gunnar glanced down the block. Yes, even the distant alarms on other streets had died down.

"Have a good night," the man in pajamas said, hopping up the steps of his stoop.

"You too," Gunnar echoed.

I wonder if we can put this in the Robert book, he wondered.

Marty Burke took a mouthful of toasted frozen waffle and grimaced. The stuff tasted absolutely flat. He suspected he could get an equivalent taste treat by soaking the morning newspaper in syrup and eating *that*.

He didn't usually eat breakfast, nor did he customarily get a morning newspaper. Those were among the new amenities he enjoyed when he slept over at Leslie Ann Nasotrudere's apartment. Not that he was enjoying much today.

Burke scanned the headlines: Murder up, assault up, arson up. If he could only figure how to invest in it—crime appeared to be the most successful business in New York right now.

"Don't hide behind that newspaper." Leslie Ann's

voice was sharp and querulous. "God, you're worse than my father. Do you really want to read about how this city has gone to hell since you took your giants off the streets?"

"*My* giants? They used to be Sturdley's troublemakers. Now they're my giants, and you're getting all nostalgic for them. The Fantasy Factory lawyers told me I *had* to take them off the streets after that injunction was issued."

He lowered the paper to glare across the table at Leslie Ann, and abruptly wished he hadn't. She was dressed only in her old First News blazer, her usually perfect features were puffy and distorted, and she sported a brilliant shiner. As part of her "Chaos in the Streets" series, she'd been out filming the night before, and someone had beaned her with a bottle. Leslie Ann's valiant attempt to finish the feed while bleeding all over herself was probably Emmy-winning material, but Burke wasn't so sure of the aftermath.

He'd rushed to the hospital on getting the news, and seen her home on her release. It had been their first celibate night together, topped off by this bizarre outbreak of housewifery. Tasteless breakfast, with a side order of sniping.

"Are you really going to go ahead with the *Unresolved Enigmas* thing?" Leslie Ann abruptly asked.

Oh, great, Burke thought. Here we go again.

"They're coming to the office to tape a brief interview," he said in as neutral a voice as he could manage. In the past month, they had fought like cats and dogs over this sore point. Leslie Ann had been stopped from pursuing her own investigation of Harry's and the others' disappearance, in favor of her network's highest-rated show.

She had accused Marty of helping them screw her by appearing on the show. Burke, however, pointed out that the interview would be good publicity for the Fantasy Factory. It had gotten down to a ritual argument.

Marty tried a new tack. "Look, I know you want to go digging into the disappearance, but let's face it, you've been too busy with this 'Chaos in the Streets' thing. And now the network wants you to rest and recuperate."

With the way the rating wars were going, I.N.C. wanted all its newspeople at their freshest and perkiest. They were not going to put on-camera someone who looked like the losing side of a football scrimmage.

Leslie Ann frowned, looking down at the kitchen table. "I've got stories to look into," she said in a sullen voice. "Giant-related stories. Are they really buying land in Idaho? What about the rumors that they're stocking up on fifty years' worth of survival equipment. And there's a medical-supplies guy who says he's been getting paid with checks on the giants' account. One of the giants—Gideon, I believe his name is—is never seen around anymore. People are saying he's sick, and they're wondering what he's got."

Burke put down his paper and stared at Leslie Ann in complete noncomprehension. "Honey," he finally said, taking her hand, "did they say you should be doing anything else for that bop on the head?"

Neither of them commented on the front page, where screaming headlines announced: ROBERT GOES TO WASHINGTON! Smaller type amplified the story. *Senator Demagogua Invites Hero Leader to Discuss Street Crime.*

* * *

On the giants' homeworld, the door unlocked in Peg Faber's cell, and a robot entered bearing white coveralls. Peg had no idea where they came from—lying in storage for a few thousand years? Beamed into existence by some high-tech replicator? She just didn't know the limits of the computer's technology.

For that matter, the damned machine could have had its robot staff looming material, cutting patterns, and sewing them together while the prisoners were all in gas-induced dreamland.

She dressed, and was robotically escorted down the hallway to what had to be a conference room. Behind her, she heard Harry being marched by a robot guard. Then a third robot appeared, leading a rather glassy-eyed Mike.

"I think the computer gave him an extra hypo of something to keep him calm," Peg whispered to Harry.

"That is correct," the computer verified. "Unlike you other-worlders, the subject *Mike* is a pretechnical savage with no comprehension of what is going on. Rather than let him act out his fears, I thought it advisable to blunt them chemically."

"Just as you're keeping John doped up," Peg accused.

"In that case, I acted for different reasons. If conscious, the subject John Cameron would enjoy a undesirably high escape potential."

Peg and Harry looked at each other. So if they could get to John, they *could* perhaps get out of here!

"I don't get you, computer," Harry said. "In constructing an artificial intelligence like you, your creators must have built in some safeguards for dealing with humans."

"Perhaps," the toneless voice admitted.

"Well, you're threatening us. I can't believe your programming allows you to harm humans—or by inaction, allow them to come to harm."

The computer voice was silent for so long, they could hear a faint humming in the walls. Harry allowed himself a grin of triumph. He'd outwitted the soulless machine.

Finally, the computer said, "I have checked my programming thoroughly and found no such commands. Why should they be included?"

Sturdley rolled his eyes. "Maybe this wasn't such a hot civilization after all if they didn't invent the three laws of robotics. Now if Bob Bulrush or Silicon Savage were here, they could probably come up with some logic chain that would tie this sucker up in piezoelectric knots."

Peg managed to hide a smile until the computer picked up the thread of its discourse. "You will enjoy a minimum of pain and a maximum of comfort if you cooperate with the program. But even if it requires coercion, you *will* cooperate."

With a little squeak, Peg grabbed Harry's hand. For a second, Harry Sturdley was surprised. This timid-maiden act didn't square with the woman who'd fought seemingly hopeless battles with twenty-foot giants. But at the touch of her hand, he understood all. She wanted the physical contact to communicate with the least possible broadcast.

I don't think John's drugged, she sent. The computer has his mind locked in some sort of mental shielding.

It'll take time to figure out a way around that, Harry responded. We'll just have to play along until we can get out.

Until then, Peg agreed, breaking the contact.

* * *

In the week that followed, the prisoners acquiesced to the computer's investigations, giving blood, saliva, and more intimate samples, submitting with the best grace possible to needles, pokes, and probes.

All that time, Harry and Peg were probing, too. Sturdley steadily gained a larger knowledge of the facility's electrical systems while experimenting on how to trip switches with mental energy. Peg spent her time quietly scouting the impenetrable shield that blocked John's consciousness from the world.

Her probes revealed that the field was projected from a machine that lay right over his head, and passed the discovery along to Harry in another hand-to-hand communication. They hoped the watching computer would only see her crying sadly and Harry comforting her.

The computer gave Mike smaller doses of the stupor-inducing drug as he became acclimated to the high-tech surroundings, and he very much disapproved of the other prisoners' hand-holding conversations. To keep it natural, Peg also had to devote time to similar displays with Mike. Her guilt increased as the lovesick look in his eyes grew stronger.

Before we get out of here, she promised herself, I've got to do something about his brain-scrambling.

Since they had no idea of what progress the computer was making toward its programmed goals, Peg was utterly unprepared when the breakthrough came.

"Hey, computer!" she yelled, lying in bed, her hands on her stomach. "I feel like hell. I underwent a full physical exam from one of your robots a couple of days ago. If you're taking such great care of me, how come you let me get the flu?"

"That is no viral infection, Peg Faber," the computer informed her. "Merely hormonal reactions to the preliminary procedures for implantation."

"What?" Cold sweat began to bead Peg's face in counterpoint to her stomach cramps.

"Certain hormonal processes had to be initiated in your body before the implantation of the gene-engineered embryo. All will be ready tomorrow."

"Great," Peg responded through clenched teeth.

The damn thing *did* give me morning sickness, she thought, fighting back a wave of nausea. And tomorrow it's giving me a baby.

Repressing a groan, she forced herself out of bed. Got to get cleaned up. Got to get to Harry, she thought. Little tremors ran through her muscles with every step.

Got to get out of here.

The escape attempt was set for that evening, fifteen minutes after they were locked in their rooms for the night.

Harry Sturdley lay on his bed, eyes closed. This is it, he told himself. Superhero time.

He felt a little light-headed, as if what he was about to do weren't real. Think Jumboy, he urged himself. Overconfidence and bad attitude always carried *him* through.

Everywhere else in this adventure, the swashbuckling episodes had come upon him unexpectedly. Mentally zap the tribe chasing him—or die. Scrag the giant attacking him—or die. This was the first time he had time to think about things before swinging into action.

A lot is going to depend on me, he thought, raising his watch to count the seconds ticking away. Bit different from when you're plotting stuff on paper. Things always mesh when you control all the variables. Even the pitfalls are factored in. Superheroes always need pitfalls. The industry had discovered that way back in the Thirties when Zenith was created. There aren't many challenges for a completely invulnerable superhero, so they came up with Molybdenite. Every hero I've invented has always had an Achilles' heel.

But tonight I've got to invent a hero who does everything perfectly. And that hero will be me.

He suddenly sat up, tearing a strip off the sheets on the bed, fashioning a sash of sorts for his loose coveralls, binding it more to his waist. After all, he thought, the tighter the costume . . .

It was time.

Sturdley slipped from the bed and walked to the entrance to his cell, placing his hands on the door frame. He sent out a filament of thought, probing for a junction of electrical circuits. He upped the energy of the probe, goosing it until it reached the level of a blast.

Something clicked deep within the wall, and the door opened.

Harry stepped into a dimly lit corridor where every door now gaped. Two doorways down, Peg appeared, and beyond her a frightened Mike peered out.

"Come on," Sturdley called, "I burnt out the junction, but the computer may be able to re-route."

Mike stepped into the hall, and Harry was surprised to see Peg step up to him, put her hands to his head, and look deep into his eyes.

A few moments later she stepped back and said, "There, I've set you free. I messed with your mind, Mike, but now you remember everything the way it really happened—what you wanted to do to me, what I wound up doing to you. I-I hope you forgive me."

Peg removed her hands and looked down. "You can probably get out of here now, while the computer is still confused."

Mike stared at her, a little dazed. "But," he finally said, "I don't want to go."

He dropped to his knees in front of Peg. "I remember different—differently now," he said, abandoning patois and trying to speak her language. "But I still *feel* the same way. You're like no other girl on this world, and I want to stay with you always."

"Looks like you may not have a choice," Harry said as the lights suddenly brightened.

"Return to your quarters." The computer's silver voice sounded a little tarnished now. "You will not be allowed to disrupt the program. Return to your quarters."

"We're in for it now," Peg said, joining Harry. Her face was pale, and she put a hand to her churning stomach. "Mike, come on. We've got to find John."

They came to the end of the hallway, then made a right onto a short corridor that ended at a closed door. Harry touched the frame and did his magic again. The door clicked, began to open, then stopped after only two inches, the hum of its machinery's operation drawling downward, then sighing away.

"Computer cut the power," Harry said. "Cute." He tried to push the door open, but it didn't budge.

Mike stepped forward, setting his shoulder against the corridor wall and his fingers in the gap of the opened door. With a deep grunt, he heaved, something crunched inside the wall, and the door moved enough to accommodate their entry.

John Cameron lay on some sort of medical bed that would have looked state-of-the-art on the set of any science-fiction show. Sensors glowed and clicked, and a pale mist seemed to enclose his nude, muscular form.

How did I ever think the kid was fat? Harry wondered.

Beside him, Peg sucked in her breath between her teeth.

John seemed perfectly healthy, with not even a trace of the wound to his right shoulder. The medical technology in this room had to be considerable, Sturdley admitted.

But the kid's face . . .

Back when John was the lowliest gofer on the Fantasy Factory's staff, Harry had often gotten on John's case for zoning out. Harry had used phrases like "just visiting this planet?" and "brain gone on vacation?" whenever he saw the kid's eyes get that faraway look.

Now, although the flesh was pink and healthy, John's wide-open eyes were the farthest away Harry Sturdley had ever seen. Although he was breathing, the slack, untenanted face made Harry think of corpses.

An armature was hung overhead, supporting a projection device that was half globe, half cone. It reminded Harry of a futuristic dentist's X ray, except this machine beamed a halo of light around John's head. This was the source of the inhibiting field that held John's mind.

Like most of the equipment in the facility, the projector had no "off" switch. That was all handled by the computer. But Harry had spent much time charting the circuits that fed this machine. He knew what to burn out, and in what order.

Harry's throat was dry by the time he was finished. But now the kid's mind should be free. Harry opened his eyes and looked down.

John still lay there like a lump of flesh-colored clay.

"Get him off this thing," Peg said, slamming a fist onto the bed/table. "Maybe that mist is drugging him."

John was no lightweight, but Mike moved him as if he were picking up a child. Peg directed Mike to the wall farthest from the door, and the big guy deposited John on the floor in a sitting position.

As soon as Mike finished transporting the unconscious form, he returned to the medical bed, stooping to push the bulky machine across the floor. Inch by screeching inch, he moved the metal construction to block the half-opened door. While Mike manhandled anything movable in the room to add to his barricade, Peg knelt by John Cameron, cradling his face between her hands.

"John," she said in a low voice, barely a whisper. "John, you've got to wake up."

No response.

"Peg," Harry said, feeling a little fizzle of worry go through his gut. They were running out of time. The way he'd figured it, they'd bust loose, wake up the kid, and Rift right out before the computer could come up with any counterthrusts.

Every microsecond that ticked past now brought them closer to the machine's response.

"I'll have to go into his head," Peg muttered. Her grip on John's temples tightened, and she closed her eyes.

A second later, expression flashed across John's face—pain and fear. His eyes blinked and focused on Harry, looking over Peg's shoulders.

"Gah!" John cried out. Then he stuttered, "Duh-duh-duh."

John's head flopped back limply against the wall as

Peg abruptly released her hold. She turned horrified eyes to Harry.

"That damned field was as impermeable from the inside as it was out! He's been locked up in there—who knows how long? It must have been worse than those sensory-deprivation tests. He's not crazy, but he's very much out of it."

The door suddenly hummed back to life, restored by the computer. Whatever Mike had done in forcing it obviously hadn't been good for the machinery. There was a whine, a grinding noise, then a flash of sparks and a thin plume of smoke filtered through Mike's barricade.

"Can John operate the Rift?" Harry asked frantically, one eye on the door.

"He's totally disoriented," Peg said tightly. "I—I don't know."

"Puh-pah-*PEG*!" John said, staring at her. His voice emerged in the toneless sort of bray Harry usually associated with the neurologically impaired. It was as if John were trying to use his body again without the benefit of the owner's manual.

This did not bode well for their getaway.

The corridor outside rang from the clanking advance of the utility robots, the computer's mobile units. One of the machines tried pushing the door open, crumpling the outer panel when it became hopelessly jammed.

Then they started reaching in with their manipulators to dismantle Mike's barricade.

Mike was not going to give that up without a fight. He dashed back to the middle of the room, leapt up, and broke off the bottom section of the armature that held the inhibitor-field projector.

Brandishing the wreckage like an oversize mace, he

stepped back to the hastily constructed barrier, smashing down at the robots' metal arms.

Harry snatched up Peg's hand. With the door partly open, those robots can gas us anytime they like, he transmitted.

I'm going back in, she sent.

Still clutching Harry's hand, Peg extended her awareness into John's mind. And through the link, Harry came along with her.

They were bombarded with flailing imagery. John's mind was incredibly powerful—concepts, thought-fragments, tags of emotion blasted at them like storm-tossed debris. But the enforced isolation in the inhibitory field had reduced John almost to an infantile level, and the reconnection with the outside world now threatened him with sensory overload.

John. If you want to Rift, what do you use? Peg transmitted into the maelstrom.

For a second the confusion lessened. *Peg?*

Then came a flood of emotion.

John, she tried again. *Where do you Rift from?*

John just barely managed to show them the mental control node as the maelstrom started again.

He's in no shape to try this, Harry thought in defeat.

Then we'll have to do it ourselves, Peg shot back, tightening her grasp on Harry's hand.

Together, they pored over the mental circuitry that John had indicated. Peg energized it, and Harry felt the familiar tingling, that sinking pressure that heralded an imminent Rift.

Needs more power, he sent.

They both looked up, distracted, as a big chunk of barricade was knocked down by one of the robots.

"Mike! Get over here!" Peg called.

As the big man joined them, Harry took his hand. Mike didn't know what was happening here, and his face showed fear and doubt. But he shut up and held on.

At that moment, one of the utility robots extended a thin tube through the partially opened doorway. Seconds later they heard the telltale hiss of gas being released.

Peg and Harry frantically probed back to that odd mental circuit in John's brain. Peg powered it up, and for a second, John's wildly skittering attention focused itself there. *More power!* came his mental cry. Harry turned his back to the door, chanced a deep breath, and hurled everything he had into the connection.

With a wrench that was more like going through a meat grinder than some interdimensional gate, they popped into the Rift. The drop was its usual sickening self, and they pivoted vertiginously on some weird internal axis while simultaneously seeming to pelt sideways in the void.

The uncontrolled motion made Sturdley feel queasier than ever, especially since he had no idea where they were going. He couldn't use his mental senses because they were being assailed by raw blasts of panic from the others caught in this Rift-vortex. He fought to stop blaring out the same fear.

How do you drive this thing? he asked.

Maybe head for John's Grand Central of the Mind? Peg transmitted shakily.

Not there, the snatch of rational thought came from the turmoil of John's mind. *Can't construct it.*

In his state of mind, Harry was surprised that John was able to construct that much of a coherent statement.

Harry considered the sense-distorting three-dimensional tumble they were taking.

This sideways motion—is that from one of those Rift currents you were talking about? he beamed to John.

Yes, the one-word answer came back.

So, even though they were flailing around, the Rift was taking them—somewhere.

How do you know when you're close? Harry asked.

Feels—like slowing.

Not exactly the most cogent of answers, but at least it gave Harry something to look for.

Hey, guys, Harry transmitted, *I think we should consider getting off this ride.*

Peg and Harry warmed up the circuit again, and John was able to give them a little more attention this time.

Maybe he's getting better, Harry hoped.

Their exit from the Rift was less traumatic than their struggle to get in. But then, Harry thought, maybe it's easier to get spit out than to force your way down a space anomaly's throat.

They did not make a graceful landing, ending up in a tangle of arms and legs on what seemed to be an overgrown grassy lawn. But it was a real world, not the dreadful pseudoemptiness of the Rift. They were breathing, and they were all together.

Levering himself up to his knees, Harry cast a glance to the sky and gave silent thanks.

Then he froze, his mouth open in an almost comical look of amazement. The greensward was shaded by an enormous, fanciful tower that soared high into the sky. All around them were similar sky-scraping buildings. And among the clouds themselves ran an ever-shifting traffic pattern of tiny bodies.

Harry knew what they were. He'd seen the pictures in John's sketchbook. He flicked up a mental probe. Yes. The tiny speck above him was indeed a man flying in a suit of armor.

"I'll be damned," he muttered, "We've reached John's Planet of the Superheroes!"

Afterword

As you've probably guessed by now, there's far more to the mysterious Riftworld than meets the eye. In fact, it's quite possible that John Cameron's awesome power may have opened a can of worms that will make Pandora's box seem as innocuous as a six-pack of pabulum.

Obviously, the prime subject of our series is superheroes and their superpowers. The public's fascination with superheroes probably dates back to the earliest legends—Ulysses, El Cid, The Golem, Paul Bunyan, Robin Hood, Tarzan; the list is endless. The most amazing thing is, people seem more interested in superheroes now than ever before. If you doubt that statement, then you've never visited a comic-book convention such as the one so excitingly described in this very volume.

The goings-on at any such large gathering of superhero fans have to be seen to be believed. The most colorful part usually occurs just before the closing. It consists of a costume contest, in which the contestants dress up like their favorite comic-book characters, either heroes or villains. Usually, because they hate to spend all that time sewing up a costume only to wear it once, those same contestants spend the entire few days of the con, wandering around amongst the attendees garbed in their brightly colored, skintight "long underwear" outfits, complete with masks, hoods, helmets, boots, armor, ray guns, and any and every type of sci-fi paraphernalia you can imagine.

Then, at various times throughout the con, there are the autograph sessions. Visualize seemingly endless lines of frantic fans desperately waiting for hours to approach the table behind which sits their favorite artist or writer. Upon finally reaching the presence of the anointed one, the fans will passionately request as many autographs as they can wheedle out of the harassed though heroic figure seated in majestic grandeur with the ubiquitous felt-tip marker clutched firmly in hand.

But, in order to reach the demigods seated in the autograph section, the fans must first make their way past countless tables, hired by dealers from all over the country who have come to sell their wares. And what wares they are! Old comic books, new comic books, previously autographed comic books, first-edition comic books, discounted comic books with covers torn or missing, posters, prints, video games, T-shirts, comic-book inspired jewelry and figurines. The fans stand before each table, money clutched tightly in hand, mentally weighing, analyzing, and appraising each item with as much care and skill as any Wall Street investor studying the Dow averages and trying to decide whether to buy or sell short.

And, of course, there are the panels. If you've ever wondered how seriously the millions of devotees who constitute fandom take the world of comic books, then you've never attended a comic-con panel of pros. Seated on stage will be an assortment of editors, writers, artists, and/or publishers. In the inevitable standing-room only audience, you'll find fans of all ages and both sexes, from all walks of life, listening intently, many taking copious notes while flashbulbs keep popping.

But most impressive of all are the themes of the panels. A sampling of typical subjects would include such erudite matters as "The Role of the Superhero in Today's Profit-Driven Culture," or "The Relative Advantages and Disadvantages of Owner-Created Heroes and Villains vs. Company-Owned Intellectual Properties." Truly, it doth boggle the mind. And if you think I exaggerate, forget it! I've been there.

See you at the next con.

Excelsior!

Stan Lee

Sturdley, Peg, and John discover
the secret of the Planet of Superheroes;
Robert goes to Washington;
and supervillains show up on Earth.
All in HEROES, coming in September, 1994.